FANNY AND THE MYSTERY IN THE GRIEVING FOREST

FANNY AND THE MYSTERY IN THE GRIEVING FOREST

RUNE CHRISTIANSEN

TRANSLATED FROM THE NORWEGIAN
BY KARI DICKSON

Book*hug Press

Toronto, 2019
Literature in Translation Series

First English Edition
original text copyright © 2017 by Rune Christensen
English translation copyright © 2019 by Kari Dickson

Published originally in Norwegian under the title *Fanny og mysteriet i den sørgende skogen* by Forlaget Oktober AS, 2017. Published in agreement with Oslo Literary Agency.

This translation has been published with the financial support of NORLA

Book*hug Press acknowledges the land on which it operates. For thousands of years it
has been the traditional land of the Huron-Wendat, the Seneca, and most recently, the
Mississaugas of the Credit River. Today, this meeting place is still the home to many
Indigenous people from across Turtle Island, and we are grateful to have the opportunity
to work on this land.

Library and Archives Canada Cataloguing in Publication

Title: Fanny and the mystery in the grieving forest / Rune Christiansen ; translated from
the Norwegian by Kari Dickson.
Other titles: Fanny og mysteriet i den sørgende skogen. English
· Names: Christiansen, Rune, 1963- author. | Dickson, Kari, translator.
Series: Literature in translation series.
Description: First English edition. | Series statement: Literature in translation series |
    Translation of: Fanny og mysteriet i den sørgende skogen.
Identifiers: Canadiana (print) 20190149264 | Canadiana (ebook) 20190149272
    ISBN 9781771665186 (softcover) | ISBN 9781771665193 (HTML)
    ISBN 9781771665209 (PDF) | ISBN 9781771665216 (Kindle)
Classification: LCC PT8951.13.H45 F3613 2019 | DDC 839.823/74—dc23

Printed in Canada

Reality, or certainly whatever pretends to be reality, came back.

PIERRE MICHON

DEATH

Slowly, slowly. All that effort. Nothing happens on its own. Neither the unflagging sun nor the most unobserved life in the depths of the ocean was created without effort, without forbearance. A badger looking for a home under the span of a bridge, the stones and clay that force their way up through the soil in plowed fields, the wood that warps and then sighs in the interior of a house, all are unaware of their own patience.

I no longer remember the circumstances, but once when I was young, I claimed it was possible to work out if two people, two strangers, would meet one day. It was simply a matter of mathematics, I believed. This statement flew out into the room like, more than anything, a winged insect with beautiful antennae. Of course it was just nonsense, of course I was just fibbing, telling comforting tales at best, as it is instead the end that can be calculated, the separation that is inevitable and to be counted on.

Let me tell you a story: a woman and her husband were in a car accident. The day was waning, they were on their way home from a shopping centre, and for some unknown reason, the car swerved off the road and straight into a transmission tower. The man's life was not to be saved, and the woman lay in hospital for a week before she too died. They left behind a seventeen-year-old daughter, Fanny, the only remaining person in an otherwise childless branch of the family, and as these tragic events unfolded, autumn swept in with weeks of incessant rain and soon the corn stood rotting in the fields.

Despite her young age, Fanny was allowed to stay on in her childhood home. The months passed, and grief kept her company, it belonged to her, like her crooked nose, the colour of her eyes, and the shape of her fingers. It was both a strenuous and an undemanding time there in the old house. Fanny did as best she could, it was nothing special, she thought: getting to school, repairing the eavestrough, chopping wood, and weeding.

One morning she was woken by strong winds that had forced the birch trees out in the yard to sway so wildly that the tips of the branches whipped and knocked at the eavestrough. And when she realized there was no chance of going back to sleep, she kicked off the duvet and swung her legs round to sit on the edge of the bed. She folded her hands, not to pray, but to listen. Was there a fox rummaging in the garbage bins out there? It reminded her of the evenings when her mother had rattled through the kitchen cupboards looking for whatever whisk or pan she needed. Her mother, who had left her in the lurch there in the pallid light of the hospital, after she'd shouted, no, screamed, that it was sentimental and sick to sit by a bed and wait for someone to die. Her crazy, terrified mom. With youthful curiosity, Fanny had asked her straight out what she was afraid of. Didn't Fanny know? It was death. Her mother feared death. Not death per se, not death as a fact, but her own death, her own demise. There, she'd said it: it was the inevitability, that was what her mother feared.

Fanny was struck by how vague her memories of that sad time after the accident were. Her mother's face was strangely blurred. It was as though the memory had been diluted, water-logged, was no more than an unclear replica. And her father? The same was true of him. He was constantly travelling, she remembered that, he always had something to do. But sometimes Fanny saw her parents in dreams, sometimes she caught a glimpse of them, both so alive, in a town she had never been to, an imagined town, but still clearly a town with busy streets and green parks and fountains and cobbled squares bustling with people going about their business. These visions were an odd relief: a flock of pigeons taking flight from a busy marketplace, schoolchildren playing in front of a newspaper stand, and an airplane flying overhead, on its way to who knows where. But the pleasure was transient, and soon everything was fluid again, reset, forgotten.

The strange thing was, on the rare occasions that Fanny did think about the circumstances surrounding her parents' death, she always felt so in control, so balanced, despite the pain it caused, and whenever she later saw them—in her dreams, that is—it was as if the classic ghost motif had been turned on its head: it was she, the living, who was haunting the dead, she who disrupted and changed their reality, like a phantom, like a ghost in their existence on the other side.

Slightly irritated by the rude awakening, Fanny got up from the bed and stood by the window. There was a pile of logs in front of the outhouse that needed to be split and stacked. They were wet, and it would take time and energy. But Fanny was good with an axe and saw, and fortunately, the logs had already been cut to the length she wanted. Twelve inches. Perfect for the stove upstairs and the fireplace in the sitting room. "The sitting room" was something she'd inherited from her parents; the names and notions that had been attached to the various rooms and surroundings remained with Fanny, even now that she was alone in the house.

Her mother, and thus Fanny too, came from one of the oldest families in the area, but that had not resulted in prosperity or fame. They came from an industrious, stable, and, not least, settled family. After all, Fanny did not come from noble stock, but rather from people of modest means: lumberjacks, miners, and sheep farmers, and more recently: dairy employees, artisans, and the odd teacher. They were solid and reliable, one and all, and did not feel the need to travel. But Fanny broke the mould, she was restless and enterprising, and she liked to travel: already as a fifteen-year-old, she had spent the summer cycling alone around Jutland, and the year after, she travelled to southwest England, also alone.

Fanny stretched, yawned loudly, and leaned her forehead against the glass, stood like this and tried to find her way back into her dream. Was it not something about space and a star that went out? No, she had to get a move on. She put on her raincoat and rain boots and went out. She left the front door open to air the house for a bit, and got started on the wood. It was easier work than she had feared, and she was very methodical, carried the chopped wood into the outhouse and stacked the logs against the wall, because she didn't want any sticks of wood left lying around outside.

When she had finished, she hung the axe back in its place and stood looking at the house. It was long and narrow and high. The white paint had blistered on the east wall and was flaking, but it had been like that for as long as she could remember, and the building was otherwise in good condition. The gables stretched up to compete with the trees, the windows reflected the green hillsides, and if you went up into the loft or stood on the slope behind the outhouse, you could glimpse the large lake that stretched along the bottom of the gentle valley.

Fanny had left her bedroom window open upstairs. She heard some irregular bumps and thumps inside the house. She took a few steps back and stretched her neck. A deer appeared in the open window. It paraded hesitantly, erratically, almost fearfully back and forth up there. Then it stuck its head out and sniffed the air. They looked at each other, Fanny and this creature of the forest. How had it got in? And how would she get it out? She didn't want to risk meeting the animal on the stairs. Perhaps she could throw a stone or a stick at it. Surely the poor thing had some kind of instinct that would help it finds its way out to freedom again? If it was frightened enough, it would surely escape danger. Fanny looked around, snatched up a stick, and waved it at the animal. But the deer didn't seem the least bit worried. Fanny ran a few steps and threw the stick up toward it. The animal bolted away, and immediately there was a crash in the room, a crash followed by a loud thump. Then the deer came sailing out the window. With its eyes open wide and tongue flapping from its mouth, it hit the ground. Something crumpled in the dazed body, then it lunged forward without force, tried to run off, to escape, but didn't manage. It looked like it wanted to roar, but all that came out were some pitiful moans from deep in its throat. Fanny closed her eyes and put her hands over her ears, but nothing changed, nothing disappeared, it was as though all the sounds reverberated in her head, as though the pain spilled over into her where she was standing. The deer kicked and flailed. Fanny breathed in, but not out, quick intakes into her lungs. When she finally managed to pull herself together, she went back to the outhouse to get the axe. The head of the axe smelled of fresh resin. Without hesitating, she took hold of the handle, swung her arms up into the air, and with single-minded force she struck the animal's head with the sharp edge. And in an almost unbroken movement, she then threw the weapon down and fell onto the dirt beside the animal. She recognized the metallic smell from the times she'd had a nosebleed. She often did in summer, in the dusty heat, it was probably some kind of allergy, her eyes always stung in the sun. She looked at the dark hole in the deer's skull, something glistened in the deep wound. What was the point in going into an unknown house? What was to be gained by poking around and wandering up a dodgy staircase? Fanny laid her hand on the animal. Some flowers, some sweet-scented flowers, if you smell them long enough, until the initial rapture has faded, bring to mind death and decay.

A FRIENDSHIP

Once a week, generally on a Saturday morning, Fanny helped out in the church. It was the parish priest, Tobias Alm, who had suggested it. He had confirmed her, and conducted her parents' funeral. Fanny had bumped into him in the vegetable section of the local shop. He asked if she wanted to earn a little extra money. And even though Fanny suspected that he was doing her a favour, that he didn't actually need help, she said yes. The job was simple enough: there was no caretaker, so she swept the floor, ran errands, made sure there were fresh flowers in the two silver vases on the altar. She hung up the psalm numbers on the wrought-iron hooks by the pulpit and got the hymn books ready. There were all kinds of chores, the kind that quickly become routine. Fanny liked these set tasks, and the hours in the church were always pleasant. From the time she put her headphones and coat down on a chair in the vestry, until she cycled home again when she was done, she was in balance; for a while, everything that weighed her down was lifted. Her parents had never had much of a relationship with the church or religion, and nor did Fanny, to be fair, but after she started working for Alm, she started to say a prayer every evening. She didn't give it any thought. It just happened. Perhaps it was the minister who had awakened this in her. Even though he never talked about such things, she picked up bits and pieces when he ran through his sermons, from the psalms he always sang, the scriptures he mumbled. She didn't know much about him, other than that he had written a couple of books, novels apparently, and that he had been a communist—well, a socialist at least—before studying to become a minister. He had been friendly and open-minded with Fanny when she was preparing for confirmation; she was often not there, but he had turned a blind eye and did not register these absences anywhere.

Alm had a scar on his left cheek. Fanny noticed it when they were rehearsing for communion. He leaned forward, and in the bright sunlight that flooded in through the side windows, she noticed the white line on his otherwise weathered face. Almost as though an axe or a sword had struck his cheek, she imagined. It looked deadly, and she was intrigued, but could not bring herself to ask. She let it go, despite the discovery having as good as stared her in the face. She was certain it had been a fateful event.

The same evening, before sleep took her, Fanny imagined all kinds of scenes in which Alm's cheek had been struck: with a sword in play, a big knife in a bitter fight, a plank on a building site. It might of course have been an accident, an unfortunate episode from Alm's youth, but that didn't invoke the same horror, the same thrill. Fanny liked the minister. She liked the fact that there was a secrecy about him. How old could he be? Mid-fifties? Maybe older? Had he been married? Did he have children? She had no idea.

Every evening, before she turned off the light, Fanny sat on the edge of the bed, folded her hands, and whispered an improvised prayer, as if to show respect, respect for what she had learned, what she had overheard, what she sincerely believed to be important: "Dear God, dear creator and saviour, you who are love and miracles, bless us with your presence and grant us grace." No amen and no sign of the cross, but a little routine she had developed over time, as though to give a proper ending: she ran her finger from her forehead to her mouth and then down to her heart. Why? To signify thoughts, words, and life, that was what Fanny thought, that was what she wanted. It was a peculiar ritual, a simple gesture, because Fanny didn't actually believe in a god, she wasn't what one might call a religious person, seeking a home for her thoughts and feelings, but she was full of hope, she wanted there to be a creator, wanted there to be a saviour, hoped that that was the case. She often wondered how a person of faith viewed the world and reality. For example, what did Alm think? What did the tall, thin man think? Little was to be gleaned from their sporadic conversations. Once, as they sat on the front pews when Alm was eating his packed lunch, he told her he saw himself as a universal pessimist but a cosmic optimist. What on earth did that mean? The minister offered Fanny a sandwich, as she'd forgotten to take any food with her, but Fanny politely declined, she wasn't hungry. And the following Saturday, a rainy and windy day—when they sat down once again to eat the simple meal together and once again Fanny had not taken any food—Alm told her, as he unwrapped his sandwiches, that he had been so emotional in the past few days, which didn't happen very often, certainly not for no reason, though it did sometimes happen—sometimes he had days when he was filled by an unexpected and sneaking sadness that took hold, or perhaps, rather, he sunk into it and got stuck. Either way, it took time to shake it off, it was like a virus or an uninvited guest. But then it passed, the misery lifted, and it felt incomprehensible, distant, and soon all the miserable reasons were forgotten too. But the last few days had been different, he said, and ran his hand over his cropped hair. This time it was not the fragile state of the world that had sparked it, but rather something small and banal. He had quite randomly found himself watching a film on television, a film where Arnold Schwarzenegger played the main role. It was called *Maggie*. Had Fanny seen it? Schwarzenegger exuded such obvious power in the film, his instincts and feelings were revealed in a remarkably controlled presence, and his eyes were insistent and evasive at the same time. He paused before continuing: it was obvious that Schwarzenegger was neither acting nor reacting—he simply wanted to *be* Wade Vogel, an upright man whose daughter was going to die. And with his usual accent, for once not despite it, he was a classic hero in the unhappy tale. As he watched *Maggie*, Alm had thought of another film. He thought about Bresson's *Mouchette*. Had Fanny ever seen that? Schwarzenegger as a Bressonian model, who would have dreamed it? the minister laughed, as though he took it for granted that Fanny would know who Bresson was. But what was it that had made him think about *Mouchette*? And why was he still thinking about *Mouchette* today? Perhaps because he associated the two girls with each other, Maggie and Mouchette, because both films were so harrowing. Alm raised a hand and pointed to the crucifix on the altar. Not merciless, but harrowing, he emphasized. And then suddenly he jumped up and disappeared into the vestry. He came back with a book, which he flicked through, and then read: "For a moment, as though she was playing some terrible game, she threw her head back and looked at the highest point in the sky. The water moved treacherously around her neck and filled her ears with a cheerful buzz, like that at a party. And as she quietly twisted her hips, she thought she felt life disappearing beneath her as her nose was filled with a smell that was the smell of the grave."

Alm put the book down in Fanny's lap. It was for her. He got up again, stood stooped in the dusty dim light. He wanted to go for a walk now. Some days it helped, he said, more to himself than anyone else. And maybe, when he got to the road that ran past all the farms, past the woods and fields, he could outstrip all that was bothering him, albeit something banal, if he spotted an overgrown thistle by the side of the road, if he stopped and watched the cows grazing in one of the paddocks, or saw a bird flying overhead, something simple that distracted him and brought him joy. And maybe he would whisper to the bird or cows: there has never been any misunderstanding between us.

SHE CLEARLY
THOUGHT SHE
WAS ALONE

A couple of months after her mother and father had died, on the day it was agreed with social services that Fanny could live on her own, as she wanted, she went up to her parents' room. She looked at the objects: the alarm clock on her father's bedside table, the hair bands on her mother's. It's so spartan, almost impersonal, Fanny thought, or was it in fact deeply personal, in the way a reality can be uncomplicated, or a truth requires frankness. There was a photograph of the small family on the wall, taken on the day she came home from the hospital: a little baby in a white bonnet, with a slightly vacant expression on her face.

Fanny stripped the bed, carried the bed linen out into the bathroom, and put it in the washing machine. She wanted to make her parents' bedroom her own. She wanted to sleep where they had slept, to breathe where they had breathed, and dream where they had dreamed, as though it were possible to blend these different perspectives: her mother's, her father's, and her own. There wasn't much there to change. The bed could stay where it was, as could the two small bedside tables, which were actually two stools that had been painted white, and the yellow chair was practical, somewhere to put your clothes at night. Fanny opened the window wide, she washed and vacuumed, and then finally hung on the wall an album cover she'd found in her father's vinyl collection. There was a shark on the cover, with its mouth open wide, and in the mouth it said *inner space* in red letters. And with this alarming image above the headboard, and fresh linen on the bed, Fanny took possession of the room. She got undressed and crept in under the duvet. She thought that at some point in her life she would be so moved she would burst into tears. Only not now, not for a long time, because now she was happy. She closed her eyes and fell asleep instantly.

In the first year after the accident, her friend Margit, from the neighbouring farm, found every opportunity to go home with Fanny, and often stayed overnight. They snuggled down under the duvet on the large double bed and lay there chatting far into the night. In the morning they made coffee and breakfast, before going to school together. Fanny enjoyed these visits, she loved the uninhibited talk in the evenings. They were happy times, these evenings full of insinuations, admissions, and fun. But then Margit and her family moved to Canada. It was like a fire dying down to glowing embers. For a while they exchanged messages—affectionate messages, messages full of longing and loss—but then the messages petered out and there was no contact.

Fanny realized how tired she was when she came home from school in the evenings. How exhausted she was when she unlocked the front door. And as for the journey, she felt it was only for the sake of sleep that she went back to the house in the country. She stumbled through her increasingly difficult existence like someone who had lost track of time. But it never crossed her mind to sell the house and get an apartment in town. Not because she felt bound to the house in any way, or that by moving she would cut a more or less abstract, sentimental link to her childhood and parents. She was, on the contrary, hell-bent on not remembering, on not being filled with memories of things that had been lost.

One autumn morning, when she was in her final year at

school, Fanny woke up abruptly as though someone had shaken her roughly. The wind had made the birch trees outside sway so wildly that the branches were knocking against the wall. She kicked off the duvet and sat on the edge of the bed, barely awake. Her mother had always had the radio on to listen to the news. But it was quiet in the house now, and even though Fanny had got used to it a long time ago, she sat there for a moment, listening. Then she got up from the bed and went over and stood by the window. She yawned loudly and leaned her forehead to the glass. There was a crack in the irregular pane, a defect in the top right-hand corner. She pressed the glass gently with her finger, stood there waiting for something to happen, something normal or something shocking, anything; it was as though the defect were symbolic of something intangible, beyond possible. But she quickly realized it was nothing more than the kind of nonsense one sometimes imagines when one isn't fully rested. There was a small ball lying on the window sill, a miniature mirrored ball like those that spin above dance floors in discos. She held it in her hand, a gentle prism vibrated against her skin. With a straight finger, she started to count the small mirrors, but soon gave up. What a waste of time! She opened the window to get some fresh air. Puh, she had to have a shower and get a move on.

Later, as she stood over the kitchen counter, stirring some sugar into her tea, it struck her how little the world was affected by whether or not she existed, nothing, really, other than the sweetener dissolving in the golden brown liquid, the woollen socks that had been abandoned on the bathroom floor when she went to bed the night before, and the window latch that she secured carefully every morning—trivialities, all of them. She drank her tea in greedy gulps, put her school books in her bag, slipped into her sneakers, and pulled on her coat. As she did this, she thought about how little she remembered, that perhaps she didn't want to remember, that she had instinctively held the memories at arm's length. Something popped up, and she interrupted it by thinking about something else. But "thinking about something else," what did that mean? No matter what you thought about, you thought about something else. That was the way of the world. Wasn't it? When you stacked newly chopped wood, you immediately thought of your father. When you thought of your father, you pictured a forest path leading up a hill. One morning, when Fanny was a lot younger, just a little girl, she had opened the kitchen door and called for the dog, who usually lay under the eaves at night. It was standing on stiff legs and whimpering. But why? What had caught its attention? What had frightened the dog? She'd forgotten. Forgotten or suppressed, pushed back down. And the dog's name? Ah, she really had to get a move on now.

She had a long journey to school. First she had to cycle two kilometres to the bus stop, which fortunately had an old shelter where you could get out of the rain and snow, then it was a ten-kilometre drive to the nearest village and station, and then half an hour on the train into town. But in town, she was just like everyone else, it was as if the senses remembered less than reality there. She had no idea what the others thought about the fact that she lived so far out in the country, so far away from everything and everyone. Did they not care? Or were they just careful to avoid any conversations that might be painful? In which case, that suited her fine, because Fanny did not want to talk about her moods and emotions. Only on bad days did she imagine that the others at school, the teachers and pupils, her friends even, felt sorry for her, having to live such a miserable life out there in the sticks.

She checked that her cellphone was in her coat pocket, put an apple in her mouth, and unlocked the front door. She had left the bedroom window open. She couldn't be bothered to go back upstairs to close it. She ate the hard apple and threw the core into the underbrush.

She was on time for the train again that day too. She had travelled this route so many times, it was familiar, the open fields, the well-maintained farms, the factories along the river, the clusters of houses and woods at regular intervals. Everything was familiar and safe, and the hilltops that ran along either side of the open valley lay lethargic like a procession of dozing animals. She found comfort in these journeys; in the morning, in particular, she liked to sit with her head against the cool glass of the window, with her eyes shut and music playing in her ears. The clouds didn't care, and sailed on, undisturbed by her existence, the wind blew in gusts in the treetops and the cars on the main road were indifferent to her gaze. She thought she was the only one who was dependent on her.

WHAT PRETENDED
TO BE A
SOLAR SYSTEM

The school lay on the east side of town, opposite the train station. The brick building towered over one of the busy, narrow streets and was not in very good shape: the walls were full of cracks, and the section that faced the parking lot was covered in all kinds of cryptic signs and peeling graffiti tags; the eavestroughs were blocked with old leaves and birds' nests, so the dirty water had trickled down and stained the facade. The building had of course retained some of its former glory, but decades of decay had staked out a sorry course for the once grand and reputable seat of learning. In summer, when the only way to get any circulation in the classrooms was to open the windows, the noise of the traffic was so loud that several of the pupils wore headphones when reading and writing. As teaching was out of the question, the teachers simply gave out tasks—pupils were asked to read from this page to that in the geography textbook, to solve these equations, or to write an essay on one of the given topics in ancient history or literature, or a comprehensive argument on a political theme.

The schoolyard was surrounded by a high wall, and above the gate was a wrought-iron decoration: an elongated, ornate landscape with figures, people and animals, reaching up toward the sun. And in the sun was written *Scientia* in flaking gold letters, as though this celestial body, in some mysterious way, which was only enhanced by the Latin, represented all wisdom, all mortal experience, and mundane routine. To an unobservant eye, the building behind the high wall might resemble a miserable prison or godforsaken factory from a bygone age.

In the row in front of Fanny, by the window, sat Janos, a clever and articulate student. They had barely exchanged a word since he appeared in the class halfway through term. Fanny had no idea where he came from, no accent gave away a mother tongue other than her own, but from the start she had noticed his reserved, almost cold, manner, and the way he sat quietly until any discussion was almost over, only then to add his solemn opinions. And sometimes, when he read out something he had written, an essay or an answer, Fanny noted down the odd formulation, quite literally behind his back, not so that she could use it herself, but so she could understand what he meant, really get to the bottom of what he was saying. One such essay, a very sombre one, captured Fanny's interest in particular: Janos was reading in his even, sophisticated way about the snail, the coldest of all creatures, and how it seeks to mate, seeks contact, in order to turn away from death. Where did he find information like that? Fanny couldn't help but be intrigued by the young man. It was as though he wanted to make sure that everything could be put into words, that it was possible to name every component in the world, all existing parts and organs. But Fanny wasn't sure that was possible, because it wasn't possible to remember everything, and what wasn't remembered was lost, wasn't it, and in any case, bits of some memories were paradoxical and abstract, sensations and glimpses rather than language, not like some revelation, not like complete events that could be recaptured in words. Despite these misgivings, Fanny wished she could find a way to get to know Janos. It was impossible in the schoolyard. At break time, he was always busy with other people, besieged, he was in another orbit. In class it was the same—he worked hard, made notes, read, listened, in his own unique languid and laid-back way. And as time was allowed to elapse without Fanny expressing in any way that she liked him, let alone that she was attracted to him, it became increasingly difficult, if not impossible, to hope that the non-existent relationship would develop any further. Fanny had looked for him on the train, without any luck, they clearly did not go the same way; she had even followed him twice, to find out where he lived, but both times he'd just walked the streets, without any apparent plan or destination. But then, one afternoon, Fanny was later than usual as she had to do some errands in town, and she ran into him. She was rushing to catch the train, and when she turned the corner onto the main square, she collided with an elderly gentleman. The man let go of his umbrella, which was then lifted over their heads by a gust of wind and blown some way down the pedestrian zone. Fanny apologized, then turned around to go and get the umbrella, which had already been picked up. By Janos. He handed it to the man, who hurried on his way. So there they stood, Fanny and Janos, unable to escape each other. Janos held out his hand, and Fanny took it. She heard him say something, but didn't catch it, as, at just that moment, a van turned into the street and they had to move. A fleeting and vague thought made her recall something unpleasant: that in the old days, they tied up a corpse's chin so the mouth wouldn't be left open when rigor mortis set in. They stood there next to each other. Fanny told him her name, and Janos said he already knew what she was called. There was no irony in his voice. Fanny lived out in the country, didn't she? And she took the train? Fanny nodded, yes. Janos held out his hand again, this time to say goodbye. She was disappointed, disappointed in herself, disappointed in the young man's haste. He clearly did not share her infatuation.

While Fanny waited for the train, she stood poker-backed on the platform, shivering in the grim weather. She watched a boy desperately chase his little sister, who couldn't have been much more than two, as the girl tottered with short steps perilously close to the platform edge. Her parents reined her in now and then, but the girl always managed to escape. She obviously thought the whole thing was a daring game. Her brother shouted at her and at the two adults. He grabbed the little girl, but every time she managed to slip loose with incredible agility. Only when the train rolled into the station did the father lift up the enterprising child and carry her into the passenger car.

Fanny found herself a seat by the window. She put on her headphones and closed her eyes. Sometime later, the train slowed down, and then, not long after, it came to a complete stop in the middle of scrubland. Fifteen minutes passed, then another ten, without anything happening. Fanny turned down her music in case there was an announcement, but nothing was said. She looked around the passenger car. A young boy was sleeping in the seat opposite her, a woman was leaning over a stroller farther down the aisle, and an old couple were sitting side by side dozing.

A mist hung low over the fields. Fanny moved to another seat to try and see what was preventing them from moving. The parallel tracks lay straight and shiny on rust-coloured sleepers. Then she noticed a marshland with trees and scrubby brush close by. She pressed her forehead to the window and studied this unexpected discovery in the dark, not that there was anything unusual about wooded areas like this along the tracks, it was just that she had never noticed this particular one before, this untidy, dense tangle of trees, not here among all the orderly fields and grazing grounds. She was tempted to get off the train, to open the door, jump down onto the tracks, and climb over the wire fence into the trees.

When she finally got home, she brushed her teeth and went to bed, troubled by an indefinable tumult. She lay there with her eyes open, waiting for sleep, almost desperate, filled with this sensation that alarmed her, and the normally imperceptible transition from a state of awakeness to dreaming was now slippery and tense, and with small judders she tossed between the two. She thought about Janos. They would of course meet again as usual; the next day, in fact, they would meet in the classroom, but now the bond was of no interest, just awkward. What would he think of her? She wished she could be like a coin that had gone out of circulation and was worthless but kept appearing nevertheless.

WATER
THAT RUNS
ALL NIGHT

Where the anger came from, Fanny had no idea, but every now and then it was there, and she cursed her parents, cursed their absence as if they had abandoned her for selfish reasons, as if they had left her no more than crumbs she should happily gather up from the floor. All these more or less diffuse, rarely welcome memories that dangled in front of her nose, what good were they to her? Of what benefit were they, now that they no longer arose from happy and secure expectations? No, she would rather suppress it all: was childhood not just a sorry episode? And her youth, which would soon be over; was it not just unbearably tedious, like a dripping tap or a pipe in a wall that had sprung a leak?

A still, sleepless night, with only small intermittent puffs of moonlight through driving clouds. Fanny sat out on the front step. She had pulled on her father's rain boots and a coat. She couldn't stop shivering. Should she tell Alm that she was ever more frequently gripped by panic? If indeed it was panic that gripped her? Perhaps it was simply pining. *Talk, tell, confess,* no, it occurred to her that all these words meant the same thing, *to get rid of,* or perhaps they were all words that hungered for attention. Fanny didn't want attention. Attention was the same as having a constant eye on you, a frenetic, scrutinizing, and distrustful eye that found no rest. She lit a cigarette. The first she had ever smoked. A forgotten packet from her mother. Forgotten? She wanted to feel what it was like to inhale the smoke of tobacco and paper. A ritual. Not one to inherit, she didn't want to subject herself to her mother's habits, but rather to bid farewell, again *to get rid of*, to settle something, move on. Fully aware, she sucked down the smoke, coughed a little, felt dizzy. Her hands stopped shaking. She studied them, observed how they held the cigarette, the glowing end that tipped into ash. She started to hum, listened to the pure notes that came from her mouth, as though it wasn't her own but someone else's bewitched voice that had taken up residence in her body and was now leaking out, unhindered. And this voice, it manifested itself in the smoke that twirled in front of her face, silent and palpable rotations in the night dark. She would never think of her parents again now. Nor what was in the past. And if she did happen to think about her parents, her childhood, all that was in the past, then she would let it pass as though it didn't concern her, didn't upset her, didn't humiliate her. She would conquer her own memory. As though her memories were junk, worn-out toys, knick-knacks. Because she really didn't want to fall prey to a kind of desperation, or to the kind of grief that was like burrs on a woolly sweater, impossible to shake loose. She flicked the cigarette butt onto the ground, and went back to bed, and fell asleep almost immediately, calmed, with her face buried in the sheet.

TWO DREAMS

On Saturdays, when Fanny went to the church, Alm was at times downhearted and restless, and as they each went about their business, Fanny felt unsure as to how she should interpret his silence. But as a rule this melancholy did not last long, the thaw came, and soon they were engaged in a conversation, a conversation that, without exception, Alm had started. One of the themes of these dialogues—which were essentially monologues—was whether the world was actually developing, progressing or not. Alm had his doubts. He believed that even though people were constantly coming to new realizations, and developing new knowledge, we had lost as much, and as much had been wasted that could never be replaced. Was there, in Fanny's and Alm's times, authors of the same calibre as Proust and Colette, Kafka and Verne? And was there anything to surpass the films of Borzage and Keaton and Grémillon and Ophüls? It was impossible for Fanny to relate to all the examples Alm reeled off. When he talked in this way, Fanny felt he was not looking for understanding or agreement, but rather was a man who was down on his luck looking for the strength to go on.

But at other times, and not so seldom, Alm was in good heart and strode around in a fatherly way and crowed about how marvellously Fanny did her work. Who could keep the place as clean and tidy as she did? Who could polish the brass and silver so it shined as bright? Or he would read aloud to her, and with great fervour, as though the texts he had chosen were forgotten or newly discovered treasures he had found, and he was bringing them to life: "Tobias dug up a god. A god who had been lying with his scornful smile in the dirt for who knows how long." And in the middle of his delivery, all this verbosity, he threw in a steady stream of kind words for Fanny—praise for her hard work, that she was a blessed creature. He could call this out to her when she was in the gallery or up a stepladder brushing the cobwebs from mouldings and trim. These calls came without warning. It was such a pleasure to share these mornings with her. And every time Fanny left the church, the unpredictable priest stood in the doorway and bowed deeply with overstated gratitude.

One cold day they were standing out on the church steps. Fanny was on her way home. Alm had turned off all the lights and locked up, and said he would walk with her a way. But instead of setting off, they stood there on the steps. Dusk was falling. The sky to the west shimmered like mother of pearl. Alm squinted and pointed up at a plane that left a strange reddish streak in its wake. Something was happening down on the road. A couple of trucks were parked there. One was empty, the other full of gravel. The exhaust rose straight up in the cold air. Alm lit a cigarette. Another pillar of smoke against the sunset. In moments like this, Alm said, in such moments it's impossible not to want faith. Fanny wasn't sure what he meant. Which moment he was talking about. Was it the shimmering sky? Or the unmoving trucks on the road that sounded like generators? And did he not have faith, he was a minister, after all. Fanny asked him about this. The answer came without hesitation. Yes, of course he had faith. It was his duty to believe. He believed. He believed in what was invisible—what was not present. Fanny asked if he meant God. He meant God. But he wished he could also believe in the world, in people, in the same way he believed in God, in the same way he was able to put his trust in an inscrutable creator.

Fanny wanted to go.

They parted ways at the shop.

At night she dreamed. As she was born and brought up in the country, she often dreamed of animals. And in this dream, which was and wasn't about the minister, there was a horse. A thin, worn-out horse she had to drag along behind her through a desolate, unwelcoming landscape. But then, as at the touch of a wand, the dream changed, as dreams do, and Fanny was on the back of the horse galloping over lush pastures. With a firm hand on the reins and bridle, she guided the horse. It was as though both the wind and the sun sung in its mane. In the morning, as soon as she opened her eyes, she remembered something Alm had read to her: "Friendship? Express yourself more clearly. I have never heard that word before."

WAS THIS
THE DAY OF
THE LAST
MATCHSTICK?

Perhaps it's the case that an action or decision that can't be interpreted is worthless. Fanny switched off all the lights at the end of the day. The same ritual every evening: first the grey standard lamp in the living room, then the one on the sideboard in the dining room, which had over a hundred mirrored droplets, wafer-thin shards that trembled every time she walked past, showering light onto the floor, the walls—endlessly fascinating, like a living being. She left one of the fluorescent lights under the kitchen cupboard on, so she wouldn't need to stumble about if she woke up in the middle of the night and wanted a glass of water. Everything was the same as always, routine, only that evening something caught her eye: a nail. It lay between the stove and the countertop. It must have been lying there, hidden, for a small eternity. Ever since her father put up the little row of hooks for the tea towels and hand towels. It twinkled at her. And Fanny picked it up, felt the point, studied it as though it were a remarkable find. She took it with her into the bathroom, placed it on the side of the sink while she brushed her teeth, and as soon as she was in bed, she popped it under the pillow. Was it her father who had dropped it? Instinctively, she reached for it, held it in her hand. She wasn't going to get any sleep. She knew it already. She was used to sleeplessness. Who knows, perhaps she even courted it, she certainly never fled from it. But how can you flee from insomnia? That is like saying you can give yourself up to sleep, that it's a choice, self-willed, and thus that it's pathetic and passive simply to lie there in the dark without giving yourself over to dreams, to rest. Fanny turned on the light and examined the nail with indifference. She ran it down the thin skin on the inside of her arm, made a scratch, slowly, then another, faster, and then an even deeper one. It stung, a burning pain that eased as soon as the blood trickled out. She squinted at the nail, put it back under her pillow, turned off the light.

The morning wind blew in, the light found her. She rubbed her eyes and it struck her that she had dreamed about something that didn't concern her, or so she felt—what she had imagined really had nothing to do with her, and yet she felt out of sorts when she got up. She had been walking around in a forest, and in a clearing had come across a lifeless person, a girl of about her own age, and having stared in disbelief for a long time, for too long, she turned away and staggered home to tell her parents about the girl. But halfway down the hill, she discovered she was being followed, followed by something insane, a viscous, all-enveloping mass, and it poured down the hillside, swelled, caught up with her, pushed against her spine, hit the back of her head, thrust her neck forward so she stumbled on some loose stones. It was death that was forcing itself so mercilessly upon her, and now death wasn't anything or anyone, now death was just pitiful, poor air, barely breathable, or rather, it was like a lack of air, a lack of oxygen. Death was time in a rush or at a standstill, a strange hour that played havoc with the normal order of things and broke down all meaning, all faith. Or perhaps death was all of this at once, because it did not need to hide itself in this or that. It did not keep its distance, not even when one was a young person wandering peacefully around in the forest in a dream that had not warned of any danger, a dream that had no idea where death was, where it lived. And now death attached itself to her, now death held on to Fanny, like a sign, a black mark on the palm of her hand. She went out into the bathroom and thought: I take back everything I've said and done. No false humility, no confident conviction, just difficult, bewildering beginnings, one after the other, just decisions and effort. She washed off the dried blood and examined the thin scratches in the light. The skin around the deepest cut was swollen and warm. She turned on the tap again and let the cold water run over it. In the mirror, she was a stranger, not distorted but changed—her full lips were dry and cracked, her skin was pallid, with a bluish tinge under the eyes. Was there anything more pitiful than secret, self-inflicted humiliation? And on the early train into town, at school and later on the familiar journey home—she could feel it, she was now tormented by the need to understand. It was as though she needed both distractions and rest to be able to tell herself how closely she was connected to the nail, to the defeat it had entailed. What invites trust and spontaneous confessions more than loss and loneliness?

NIGHTINGALE, 1942

Fanny couldn't work out if it was Janos himself who thought that banalities were more genuine than all the metaphysics in the world, or if he was quoting from somewhere. It didn't really matter, that wasn't the point, after all. He was standing behind the teacher's desk. He was going to give a presentation. He clearly liked being there. Fanny had forgotten to hand anything in, and the teacher had not mentioned it. She followed Janos's movements with anticipation, as though she might read something from them, something about her, and even though she was painfully aware that it was only wishful thinking, she watched for some kind of message, be it ever so subtle and shy. Janos picked up something about as big as a medium-sized suitcase, carefully wrapped in a black plastic bag. With obvious enthusiasm, he opened out a penknife and cut the plastic. Now he had the full attention of the class. He coaxed the treasure out into daylight. It was an old reel-to-reel tape recorder. *TEAC A-3300SX*, it said on the recorder, and on the reel: *Maxell*. And then, in surprisingly few words for him, he tried to prepare his fellow pupils for the importance of what they were about to experience, and explain it to them. The class sat in silence. Fanny could feel her heart beating. She glanced around to make sure no one else could hear it. Janos started the recorder, and immediately they heard beautiful birdsong, a bird's melancholy whistles. Fanny had to turn away, her face to the wall, her heartbeat and the birdsong blended.

It went on for two minutes, and then for four, then another sound emerged from the background, quiet at first, as though hesitant, thoughtful, undecided. An airplane. Soon the thundering was massive, threatening, and almost drowned out the bird's trills. Fanny wanted to stand. She wanted to get up and go. Get up and leave the room. Leave behind all the sadness in the recording. The airplane roared inside her. She stared at the wall, her mouth filled with saliva, saliva she couldn't get rid of, couldn't swallow. But then it eventually faded out and was soon over. There was a click on the recorder. Mechanical. Liberating. The pupils sat there quietly, as though waiting for an order, a task, an explanation. With his usual authority, Janos explained that the recording they had heard was made in England on May 19, 1942, and that what they had heard was a nightingale and a Lancaster bomber returning from a raid over Germany—Berlin perhaps, or possibly Cologne. Janos's presentation was finished. He packed everything away and sat down at his desk in front of Fanny. She recognized the smell of him—the faint scent of resin. Or was it a spice. To her horror, he turned around in his chair, very suddenly, and held out an apple, asked if she would like it. She looked a bit pale, he said bluntly. Fanny nodded. But she couldn't eat more than half. Janos split the apple in two with his bare hands, then he put one half down in front of Fanny. He turned his back to her again and she heard the crisp sound of him biting into the flesh. She took a bite as well. The tart apple juice tasted good, but she was full after only one bite.

On the way to the train station, Fanny thought about the nail. The scratches on her arm were stinging. She realized that if she was sad or hopeful or overwhelmed by another emotion she couldn't counter, her appearance never gave away what she was feeling. Was it because she was shy? Or was it simply politeness, like with people who are guarded and stand on the outside of everything? Whatever the case, she believed that sorrows were something one should keep to oneself.

When she got home, before she let herself into the dark house, she thought, or rather it became clear to her, that she had not built up anything of what she had around her, she had acquired nothing. When one removed grief, there was nothing left that she could claim was hers. She chopped wood, vacuumed, washed clothes. She folded her clothes, hung them up in the normal places, tops here, jackets there, underwear in the drawer and pants folded on the shelf in the closet. The only thing she missed, the only thing she cared about in terms of loneliness, was Janos. It was an odd longing. How could she go around yearning for someone she didn't know other than as a constant reminder of rejection? In the classroom, in the schoolyard, even after his thoughtful gesture with the apple—in his presence she was someone you tossed to one side.

THE FIRST GIRL
ON THE MOON

Alm had some things he needed to do in town early, so Fanny could get a lift if she liked. As he drove, he drank coffee from a paper cup. It looked as though he was holding it in his hand to feel the warmth. His eyes were still slightly glazed from sleep, but he spoke tirelessly, all the same, about how the small and unremarkable events were what kept the world moving. Everything was connected, he believed, everything was indebted to everything else. Fanny thought it was a rather shallow view, but said nothing. She also thought that if that was the case, it would hardly be positive; to the contrary, it would fuel tyranny and dependence, a kind of ranking of fate. She imagined a group of workers installing a transmission tower not far from the highway, and a year or two after the transmission tower had been erected, for some inexplicable reason, perhaps due to a momentary loss of concentration, a car drove off the road straight into the towering steel construction. The two people in the car, a man and a woman, were taken to the nearest hospital. A doctor was working overtime in Emergency. He was missing his son's first school show. The son hadn't spoken to his father for a week. The man and the woman in the car lost their lives. Their seventeen-year-old daughter became obsessed with death. Anyone could see she was obsessed, she was certain of that, because surely it was impossible not to notice her miserable face. While Alm talked, Fanny composed a small and sorry but nonetheless clearly logical sequence: she was born + a transmission tower was raised = she lost everything. And what was the point of that? What good were the coins on the deceased's eyes and the bandage to tie up the chin? What kind of superstition was that? Was it to ensure that the dead stayed dead? Was it the desire to make sure that never again would they be able to see or speak? Was there a fear that death might leak into life? And Fanny herself, was she scared of dying? No, Fanny wasn't scared of dying. She was scared of not dying. Of being prevented from disappearing, fleeing, dissolving one day—that frightened her. Being abandoned again, left behind, only to wander around like a spirit in her own empty life, that was most terrifying of all.

Fanny leaned her head against the cold window. It was still dark outside. And it was raining, but raining without a sound. The water forced its way silently down the glass in irregular streams. She felt like an astronaut staring out into space, out into the dark mass that surrounds everything, only a glimpse of light now and then, soft sodium lighting, all distant pools and flares. She was sitting in a spaceship gliding over the surface of an unknown planet. All at once it was as if nothing weighed her down. Everything in and around her had life, as trees have life, as horses and frogs and flies do. She was dreaming. She was happy. A cascade of tumultuous time brought fragile and transparent pictures to the surface. Pockets of crystal clear, azure blue depths over the hills, the speckled darkness of the woods and forests. She closed her eyes. Alm's monologue had faded. Where did he come from? Did he have children? It was as if he carried with him the shame of a previous generation. Had he broken with everything in his former life? Former life—what did that mean?

A rabbit zigzagged across the beam of the headlights. Its graceful and terrified bounds threw long, erratic shadows over the road. Then the little beast finally jumped from the road into a ditch and out of sight.

HAPPY
CIRCUMSTANCES

October arrived. It was Sunday. A woman came cycling along the dirt road that twisted and turned along the north side of the valley like a questionable boundary between the fields and the gentle, autumn hill crests. Fanny spotted the cyclist through the kitchen window. She put the loaf down on the breadboard and followed the bike's progress. The cyclist disappeared behind the thick cluster of trees by the stream, and in a few moments would pass below the house. Fanny opened the window ajar. An aroma of rotting vegetation came from the kitchen garden: damp grass, saturated soil, dying plants. But where was the woman? Fanny leaned out so she could see better. The short stretch would normally take only a few seconds, but now nearly a minute passed before the woman reappeared. She was pushing her bike and she was limping. Even though it was cloudy and damp, she wore a simple dress and wool cardigan. There was no basket attached to the handlebars or rack, no backpack to be seen, so she wasn't going on a long trip. Fanny whistled out the window, and it was so boisterous and loud that she immediately regretted it. She wanted to pull back and hide, pretend she hadn't done it, but that would be a bit rude and, in any case, the woman had already seen her. She waved and called something that Fanny couldn't make out. Fanny opened the window wide and asked the stranger to wait.

The woman was chatty; as soon as Fanny was in front of her, she held out her hand and said, as though they were old friends, that it looked like rain, so it was perhaps best to turn back. Fanny looked at her knee. She had a hole in her tights and a graze on her knee that was bleeding. Which was a good thing, Fanny said, as it cleaned the wound. One of the tires on the bike was punctured. But that wasn't a problem, Fanny could repair it. The woman, who was a few years older than Fanny, possibly somewhere in her mid-twenties, Fanny guessed, said thank you and admitted that she wasn't very good at that kind of thing. She chatted away: wasn't it strange that the sun seemed to be so much smaller in autumn. She no doubt just imagined it, but it was so striking that she couldn't help but wonder. Yes, it was strange, Fanny agreed, the sun did seem smaller. Perhaps it had something to do with the cold air. Fanny knew that she was just humouring her, but there was something about the unknown woman that made her want to be nice. They stopped in front of the house, with the bicycle between them. Fanny went in and filled a bowl with water, got out her tools and repair kit, and then she was ready to fix the inner tube. With a screwdriver, she carefully pushed the tire to one side and pulled out the inner tube, pumped it full of air, and held it down in the water. The woman watched, wide-eyed, as though what she was witnessing was magic. There we have it, Fanny said, and pointed at the bubbles bursting out of a tiny tear in the black rubber. She dried it, sanded it with fine sandpaper and glued on a patch, and then rubbed the thin plastic film until the glue had dried. The woman stood up and once again held out her hand. Fanny had glue on her fingers, which now attached itself to the other woman's hand, but she didn't seem to notice. They introduced themselves. The woman's name was Karen. She was on her way to the lake, for no particular reason other than to get some air. She wasn't dressed for the cold weather. She lifted her head and took a deep breath. Even though there was only a light drizzle in the air, her wool cardigan smelled damp. She pointed to the ground and wanted to know what the dark patch was. It looked like blood. Karen struck Fanny as being the sort of person who would point at everything she wanted to talk about, everything she wanted to name she would point at. Fanny spotted the valve cap in the dirt, picked it up, and put it back on. Did Karen want to go and look for mushrooms in the forest with her? The question just fell out of her mouth. Fanny immediately regretted it. It was so unthought-through, almost brazen. She didn't want the woman to cycle off, not so soon, not straight away. Karen got onto her bike, put some pressure on the handlebars to check that everything was all right, that the inner tube was in fact mended. Fanny suddenly felt embarrassed, because of her question, and not least the lack of an answer. Karen mumbled that it was a shame it was too cold for a quick dip. And the fact that something had been said, it didn't matter what, this trivial statement, filled Fanny with a sense of relief. She declared that she knew a place where there were lots of chanterelles. Karen took off her cardigan. She would have to borrow some warm clothes from Fanny, a coat, perhaps. Fanny nodded. She invited Karen into the house and led the way across the gravel.

Once inside, Karen walked around looking at things, as though she was at an open house, one room after the other was inspected. What a nice home Fanny had. Was there no one else there? Was she an only child? Fanny explained briefly. Karen was not fazed in the slightest, she shook her head sympathetically and went over to stand by the window in the living room that looked out onto the raspberry bushes. She took in the view with obvious delight. Then she pointed at something again, and exclaimed: Look at that enormous flock of birds. It was so lovely, everything was so lovely, so wonderful, and wasn't it strange, that one said *a flock of seagulls* and *a school of fish*, which all seem logical enough, but then it was *a murder of crows*. Yes, it really was an odd expression, Fanny agreed. *A murder of crows*, it sounded like the title of a crime novel.

Fanny had a habit of listening to people, to complete strangers, people she had never said a word to before. With great enthusiasm she would listen to what a person who had nothing to do with her was saying, and every time, as soon as she realized she would never see this person again, she tried, with a strange affection, to master, or rather store, the tone of the person's voice. It was a rather naive pursuit, to create a kind of imitated connection, and yet this simple and thrilling observation gave her pleasure. How had things been when her parents were alive? She couldn't properly remember, but she thought they had never spoken about anything of particular interest or significance.

Not long after, the two women walked side by side up the hill. They passed among the pine trees, stepped over stones that had pushed up through the earth, and jumped over the wet hollows where coarse, twisted roots had burst free. And finally they found Fanny's chanterelles. Only a week earlier, she had inadvertently come across the culinary gold behind some felled trees. She had picked as many as she could, stuffed the pockets of her coat full, but there were still a good deal left, and with a basket each, the two women set to gathering. In her heart, Fanny was quietly bewildered by the immediate closeness she felt with Karen. She imagined that they were somehow related, certainly in temperament, their disposition at once thoughtful and spontaneous. Karen told her that she had just moved to the area, that she had bought a farmhouse she was renovating.

She said the latter with open irony. Fanny wasn't sure if this was directed at something or someone, or if she was simply hedging her bets because she knew the outcome of her endeavour was uncertain. No, Karen was just being direct, something Fanny took as a sign of trust, and this straightforwardness in the other woman meant that Fanny could reciprocate that trust. She knew this was a simple, if not downright naive, thought, but she felt it was a turning point in her life, all the same. Because one could allow oneself that, couldn't one? After all, imagining things didn't harm anyone. It was relatively uncomplicated to picture whatever it might be, and surely one could allow oneself the luxury of hope for something spectacular. There was no risk—they were doing nothing more than picking chanterelles, talking about how lovely it was here on the hillside, the colours that were still blushing and blazing, the grey sky that shone between the tree trunks. They moved around, backs bent, and exclaimed again and again what a joy it was to be able to pick so many mushrooms. They were together, like two long-lost relatives who had found each other again, and if it turned out to be their only meeting, then both of them would return to their lives having lost nothing.

On the way back, each carrying a full basket in the dark, Karen suggested they should meet again. Fanny was thrilled that this was said without any fuss, and that it had not been up to her to introduce the idea. Before any goodbyes, Karen said that the whole point was repetition, constant renewal. Fanny didn't quite understand. It was something to do with the fact that they might have changed by the next time they met. Even though it was only a matter of days, they would be transformed; as they now knew each other, they could talk together. Fanny just nodded in response to these opaque statements. What else could she do? But she was delighted that it was mutual.

FORGIVENESS

What kind of birds were they? A gust of wind shook the dew from the plum tree, and at the same time, a dozen of them flew up from nowhere. Fanny stood in the kitchen and watched the spectacle out in the garden. She had no idea what they were called; she thought with horror, at first, that they were bats—they were small and grey, and swirled around in the air before gathering themselves in a flock, which made them resemble oversized bees, and then disappearing behind the outhouse. Fanny tried to find them in the bird book her mother had once given her, when she trod on a rusty nail, but the tiny fliers could not be identified, so she gave up. She wasn't particularly interested in birds anyway.

When she got to the church, the door was open and leaves were blowing up the aisle and in between the pews. Alm was pacing back and forth in front of the altar, as he rehearsed his Sunday sermon. He had an embittered expression on his face. He mumbled: Where was it? In which gospel does Jesus say that the foxes have holes and the birds have their nests? Without looking up, he said he should have finished this long ago, but yet another service with only a handful in the congregation was anything but motivating. How could he reawaken level-headed and already reconciled believers? What could he give them other than boring confirmations? He waved at Fanny to follow him into the vestry, closed the door behind them. It was as though the silent, cool room challenged him to a reckoning, to be resolute. A reckoning with what? He balled his fist and rapped his knuckles on the old leather Bible. And with his knuckles still on the book, he expanded: every time he listened like this, every time he listened in this mighty silence, pictures rather than sounds revealed themselves, and they were always from his childhood, as though some unsolved mystery lay there. It was like dreaming about something you had dreamed. And it was of course a paradox, almost absurd, but thanks to these fantasies, these kabbalistic glimpses, as he called them, he escaped for a short time from his own thoughts, himself. He stood with his back to Fanny as he talked, but despite the fact that the message was both intense and cryptic, Fanny listened willingly. Never before had Alm shared so much. Was he having a breakdown? Was this how a psychotic person spoke? She wished he would turn around so she could read his face, his expressions, the changes in his otherwise kind eyes. But no, without turning around, he continued to confess: as a student, he was known for his rich imagination. It was a compliment always paid to him. He shook his head. Already then he had thought of imagination as an unhappy human talent, something burdensome and uncontrollable. Fanny didn't know what to say. What kind of comfort could she offer? She thought that Alm was a man who confused sorrows and deception. Yes, she thought, that was the case, even though she didn't know how much sense or realization lay in this thought. Finally the priest turned around. Fanny had to forgive him. She certainly mustn't think that anything was wrong. No, Fanny understood that he was tired. She felt an urge to pat him on the head. Alm leaned forward. He didn't blow but almost spat out the candle, and immediately it looked as though he were tumbling into an immense darkness. On the way home, Fanny thought about the deer, she pictured it clearly, leaping around in death, as elated as a summer-happy toad.

FANNY
DAYDREAMS
AT NIGHT

Fanny couldn't sleep. At the start of October, a warm, dry wind blew through the neighbourhood, followed by two days of rain, and then the landscape froze and darkened. Fanny found no peace. For several nights in a row, she lay in bed waiting for sleep, as though it were a friend who was coming to collect her, an unreliable friend who said they were coming but failed to show up. At school, she was exhausted and had to take care not to sit at her desk and doze. In the end, on the third night, when it was half past four in the morning without her having had a wink of sleep, she got up. She sat down at the kitchen table, stared at her distorted reflection in the window, and pondered, of all things, what would happen with her and Janos. Every time he said or did anything, he seemed to wait for a reaction, a consequence. Or perhaps the opposite was true—that he didn't care what the others thought or said. Whatever the case, he was himself in a way that was at once invasive and reserved. Fanny heated some milk and sat down again with her musings. And what about Karen? She had been so kind and straightforward, but now a week had passed without any word from her. In her exhausted state, Fanny wondered if the meeting with Karen had perhaps been a dream, and even though she knew that wasn't the case, the memories now resembled an abrupt series of confused longings, more than an actual event.

A large fly buzzed up from the windowsill and started to circle around her head like a small airplane. She recalled how her mother had always taken any insects that strayed into the house out onto the front step to set them free. Fanny was of a different opinion—flies and spiders had to pay with their lives. She couldn't stand the infamous pests. She grabbed a newspaper, rolled it up, and waited. As soon as the fly settled, she whacked it. And she got it the first time, and the result was a sticky mess on the cupboard door. So she had to wash over it with warm water and a cloth. The house had not been cleaned properly since her parents' death, and as Fanny liked to use wood in the fire, the damp cloth left a white streak. It looked like she'd drawn a paintbrush over the spot where the insect had ended its days. Were the walls really so covered in soot? And the ceiling? Fanny looked at the clock. She still had plenty of time. She got out a bucket, filled it with warm soapy water, and started to wash the kitchen. The cupboard doors, the countertop, and the walls were all scrubbed carefully. She pulled out the stove and the fridge, washed them down. Even the ceiling was cleaned—she climbed up onto a chair that she moved around, wiping the cloth energetically above her head. To begin with, it just looked stained, and she regretted having started, but after she had gone over it a second time, it looked clean. Dressed in her pyjama bottoms and a vest, she lay down on the floor and gazed up at the ceiling. Why did she think about Janos now as well? Why did she think he was a courageous person who she trusted implicitly? She stared up at the ceiling with an astonished, slightly scornful expression, as though she didn't quite dare to believe her own instinct. She stroked her fingertips over the three ridges on her lower arm. Examining more than caressing. The cuts were starting to heal.

There was still a little time left before Fanny had to go to the bus stop. She took a shower and got dressed. She had to go to school. She put a carrot in her lunch box, filled a bottle with water from the tap, and sat down to wait. She guessed she would be hungry when she got home but couldn't be bothered to check if there was anything in the fridge that could be made into a meal.

It was pitch dark outside and slippery underfoot, so she almost fell a few times. When she got to the bus stop, she sat down on the bench in the shelter. An unfamiliar dizziness came over her. It was as though she didn't own her body. She was confused, empty, passive. She took a deep breath. It just made things worse. Now she had to lie down. She let her body topple over onto its side, felt the cold wood against her cheek, a rough and uncomfortable bed, but it would have to do. She closed her eyes, had to smile, without knowing why. The ground shook underneath her. She had to feel with her hand. Was it she herself who was shaking so much?

She was woken by someone touching her arm. A gentle, careful hand. A person standing over her. It was an older man in worn overalls and a cap. He asked if something was wrong. No, nothing was wrong, Fanny assured him. She sat up and rubbed her eyes, yawned. The man reversed a few steps and frowned. Behind him was a red tractor. It looked majestic in the cold light. Fanny squinted at these unfamiliar figures. Was she sure that nothing had happened? She nodded. She was sure. She had been waiting for the bus and then fallen asleep. That was all. The man swung himself back up onto the tractor. Could he drive her anywhere? Then he obviously recognized her. She was the daughter of the couple who had died. It was a car accident, wasn't it? Terrible shame. She only had to say the word if there was anything he could do. Still half asleep and groggy, Fanny thanked him for the offer. It might be good to get a lift home. She climbed up onto the tractor as well, and the man started the engine. She sat so close to him that she could smell the cigarette smoke on his breath. There must have been a lot of tar in the tobacco he smoked, for it to affect his breath. The man said nothing, but the expression on his face belied the fact that he didn't quite believe her assurance, that she was hiding something from him, that something terrible had happened.

As Fanny let herself into the house, she realized she must have been asleep for a long time. She checked her phone. It had been four hours. She'd been lying in that godforsaken bus shelter for four hours. She'd lain there like a homeless person. Like a corpse. A dead girl.

The house was quiet. Only the usual wind singing down the chimney. For a while she stood listening, deep in thought. Something seemed to be approaching. A whispering roar, but Fanny couldn't decide where it was coming from, whether it was inside the house or outside. She opened the front door. The wind blew in her face, and a massive shadow slipped over the house, over the woods and fields. And just as suddenly, big hailstones rattled on the roof, against the walls and in the treetops. Fanny went out onto the gravel. She had to bend her neck to protect herself. The small balls of ice jumped around her feet. She couldn't help but laugh. She opened both her hands to the bitter, frozen rain and caught it in her palms—small bulbs of ice. The laughter came from deep in her belly: and a gasping, delirious laugh it was. She held her arms out in front of her, and the hail pelted her skin. What if this is God? she thought. What if the hailstorm was God's way of speaking? Like the plagues in the Old Testament. Perhaps this was God's way of talking to her: the clouds blowing in from the north were not snarling with anger, they were more like a subdued voice that talked of all the excess and misery that would one day come.

The hailstorm pulled away from the house and garden, and the fizzing sound faded. Fanny watched the shadow sail over the fields to the east. It had gone so far now that it had reached the top of the bank up to the road through the woods.

Could there really be a language hidden in such phenomena? No, why did she think that? Self-loathing was a feeling Fanny knew little about. She allowed herself to think whatever she liked. But what if it was all an adventure? Then perhaps it might be easier to forget the sad circumstances and to understand what the different events were actually about.

INTERMISSION
WHEN THE
TALE OF
THE HONEST
PENNY
IS TOLD

"Once upon a time, there was a poor mother who lived in a hovel some way from the village. She had little to eat and no fuel to burn, so she sent her young daughter into the forest to collect wood. The girl ran and skipped, and skipped and ran, to keep herself warm, as it was a cold, grey autumn day; and every time she picked up a branch or a root and put it in her gathering basket, she slapped her body with her arms, it was so cold, and her hands were as red as the lingonberries on the bushes she passed. When her basket was full and she was about to turn home, she stumbled upon a clearing. There she saw a twisted white stone. 'Oh, you poor old stone, how white and pale you are—you must be freezing!' the girl said, and took off her coat and wrapped it around the stone. When she came home, carrying the gathering basket, her mother asked why she was wearing no more than a cardigan against the autumn cold. The girl told her she had seen an old, twisted stone that was so white and pale with frost that she had given it her coat. 'You fool!' the woman said. 'You think a stone feels the cold? Even if it was freezing and shivering, it's each man for himself. It costs enough money to clothe you as it is, let alone when you give away your coat to a stone in a clearing'—then she chased the girl out to go and get her coat. When the girl reached the stone, it had turned and one corner was becoming uprooted in the ground. 'Oh, that's since you got the coat, you poor thing!' the girl said. But when she looked a little more closely at the stone, she saw there was a chest underneath it, full of shining silver coins. 'It must be stolen money,' the girl thought. 'No one puts money that has been honestly earned under a stone in the forest.' She took the chest down to a forest lake and threw all the money in. Only a single penny floated to the surface. 'Ah, that must be honest, for what is honest never sinks,' the girl said, and kept the coin, then took it home with her coat. She told her mother what had happened, that the stone had turned and that she had found a chest full of silver coins, which she had emptied into the lake, as it was stolen money. 'But one penny floated to the surface, so I took it, as it was an honest penny,' the girl said. 'You fool,' her mother said—she was very angry—'if only that which floated was honest, there would not be much honesty in the world. And even if the money had been stolen ten times over, you found it, and it's each man for himself. If you had taken the money, we could have lived well for the rest of our days. But you are a fool and a fool you will always be, and I will toil for you no more. Away with you and earn your own bread.' So the girl went out into the big, wide world, and she walked both far and long to find work, but no matter where she went, people thought her too small and too weak and said they had no use for her. Eventually, she came to a merchant's house, where she got work in the kitchen, carrying wood and water for the cook. She had been there some time, when the merchant made preparations to travel to foreign lands, and he asked all his servants what he should buy and bring home for them. When everyone else had had their say, it was finally the turn of the girl who carried wood and water for the cook. She held out her penny coin. 'And what would you like me to buy for that?' the merchant asked. 'It will not get you much.' 'Buy whatever you can for it, because it is honest, I know that,' the girl said. The master promised to do this, and then he set sail. Once the merchant had unloaded and loaded his ship in the foreign land and bought all that he had promised his servants, he returned to the vessel and was about to leave harbour. Only then did he remember the scullery maid's penny. 'Must I go all the way back into town for the sake of a penny? It is always more trouble than it is worth, doing good deeds like this,' the merchant thought. Just then, an old woman walked past with a sack on her back. 'What have you got in your sack, mother?' the merchant asked. 'Oh, it's nothing more than a cat; I don't have the money to feed it anymore, so I thought I would throw it in the water and drown it,' the old woman replied. 'The girl said I should buy whatever I could for her penny,' the merchant said to himself, and asked the woman if she was willing to take a penny for her cat. Yes, the old woman was quick to accept, and so a deal was done. Some time after the merchant had set sail, a terrible storm blew up, and the weather was so fierce there was nothing to be done. He drifted and drifted and did not know where he was. Eventually he came to a country where he had never been before, and he went into the city. At the inn where he stopped, the table was set with a rod for each who sat there. The merchant thought this was very odd, and he could not imagine what the rods were for, but he thought that when he sat down, he could watch and see what the others did and then do the same. Well, when the food was served, he learned what the rods were for: thousands of mice came swarming, and everyone sitting at the table had to used their rod to hit and sweep them away, and the only sound to be heard was blows from the rods, the one harder than the next. Sometimes they even hit each other in the face and had to take the time to say: 'Sorry.' 'To eat in this country is hard work,' the merchant said. 'But why don't you people have cats?' 'Cats?' they asked, as they did not know what cats were. So the merchant sent for the cat that he had bought for the scullery maid, and as soon as the cat was on the table, the mice scurried back to their holes and the people could eat in peace, such as they had never experienced. They begged and pleaded with the merchant to sell them his cat. He eventually agreed to leave it with them, but only for a hundred daler; they paid this willingly with thanks. Then the merchant set sail again; he had no more than got out to sea when he spotted the cat up the main mast, and not long after, the sea got rough and another storm blew even fiercer than the last, and he drifted and drifted until he came to a land he had never seen before. The merchant made his way to the inn, and here too was a table set with rods, only they were bigger and much longer than where he had been before. And they were needed, as there were even more mice here, and they were twice as big as those he had seen before. So once again, he sold the cat, only this time he got two hundred for it, with no haggling. He set sail, and when he was some way out to sea, there was the cat again, at the top of the mast, and immediately a storm blew up, but this time it lasted for days and days, and the boat drifted to a country where he had never set foot before. And again he went to the inn, and here too the table was set with rods, but they were an ell and a half long and as thick as a small broom, and the people said that to sit at the table and eat was the hardest chore of all, because there were thousands upon thousands of big, ugly rats, and they were lucky if they managed a bite or two now and then, as they had to work so hard to keep off the rats. So the cat was brought up from the ship again and the people were able to eat in peace. They begged and pleaded with the merchant to sell them his cat, and for a long time he said no, but then he finally promised they could have it for three hundred daler. They gave it to him gladly, with their blessings and thanks. Once the merchant was back out at sea, he thought about how much the girl had earned on the penny she had given him. 'Well, she'll get some of the money,' the merchant said to himself, 'but not all. I am the one she has to thank for buying the cat, and it's each man for himself.' But no sooner had the merchant thought this than so terrible a storm broke loose that they all thought the ship would go down. He understood that the only thing for it was to promise that the girl would get everything. And as soon as he had made this promise, the weather changed and they had a favourable wind all the way home. When he finally made land, he gave the girl her six hundred daler, and his son besides; because now the little scullery maid was as rich as the merchant. The girl lived happily ever after in love and luxury, and she welcomed her mother into her home and treated her well: 'As I do not believe it's every man for himself.'"

THANKS TO
HER DREAMS,
SHE ESCAPED
FROM HERSELF
EVERY NOW
AND THEN

What was it called? A twilight star? And if not, what would she call it? What name should she give it? Yes, a dawn star. It would be called "the Dawn Star." It hung suspended above the forest-clad hills to the north and was not exclusive to the rich and privileged. Whenever Fanny thought about the system that produced such distant wonders, she felt encouraged. Or perhaps it was just a satellite reflecting the sun. Not that it mattered, because that was also a possibility that intrigued her.

In the outhouse, she found the tools she needed to file the nail. She sharpened the point. When she was satisfied, she put it in her pocket and went back to the house.

She boiled an egg, cooled it under cold water from the tap, and ate it as she stood by the sink. She had been so composed. She had felt in control all the time. But now she was impatient, restless. She went into the bathroom, got undressed, took out the nail, and held it up in front of her. She was so pale, and the shadow of the nail on her throat was so thin.

The following night she had a dream. She dreamed she could hear the sounds of her parents in the house, a faint rustling in the walls. And everything she saw there in her sleep was real, as real as the quiet circle of light that spread out from the lamp on her bedside table, despite which she had fallen asleep, just as concrete as the comic book that had fallen onto the floor, and as tangible as the branch that once scratched her face—she still had a tiny scar over her eye, which was impossible to see unless one stood very close. In her sleep, she blew on an ember and the ember grew; it crackled, came alive, and offered up neat little flames. She could hold it in her bare hands, but then she woke up and in that moment it became a lump of coal, and when she sat up in bed and looked down at her hands, they were empty.

THE BADGER

Karen and Fanny met again quite by accident. They bumped into each other on the escalators at the shopping centre. Karen was on her way up to buy a pair of rain boots, and Fanny had been to the pharmacy to buy painkillers. Karen said she had thought about getting in touch, but the days were so full, which pleased her, as she liked working, liked getting things done, as she put it. They went out together and stood by Fanny's unlocked bike. It was raining heavily. Fanny pulled up the hood on her jacket and did the zip up to her chin. Karen offered to drive her home. She had a pickup, so there was room for the bike in the back. Fanny was more than happy to accept a ride.

When they got to the car, Karen pulled back the tarpaulin from the truck bed. Then she was at a bit of a loss, so Fanny took charge. She pushed the spare wheel to one side and lifted the bike up into the back. She was conscious that there was something quite brazen about showing off her physical strength in that way, but she couldn't help herself. Karen threw up her hands. Goodness, Fanny was so strong! For such a thin, long-limbed girl she certainly had strength in her muscles.

They didn't say much. The wiper blades swished across the windshield. Karen drove at a snail's pace, so the journey took longer—or at least, that was what Fanny thought, and it felt good to sit there with her friend. There was nothing important to be said, nothing important to be done. It was enough simply to be together in the car, in the pouring rain. When they eventually stopped outside the house, Fanny wanted to know how Karen liked living in the small farm, if she was managing to keep everything going. The questions fell out of her mouth, she asked mainly to draw out the time. No, Karen did not have animals, but she was thinking about getting a couple of horses in the spring. Fanny opened the door but stayed sitting where she was. All of a sudden, the rain stopped. She looked straight at Karen, and before she knew it she had said that she hoped Karen lived without anyone else. She didn't say "alone." She used the expression "without anyone else." Whatever the case, Fanny decided to trust that her comment would be met with understanding. Without saying anything, Karen unfastened the seat belt. In a hasty movement, she leaned forward and kissed Fanny, who immediately lifted her hand and touched her lower lip, her eyes wide in utter bewilderment. Karen kissed her again, only now Fanny closed her eyes and accepted. But then Karen had to hurry. Should they meet again soon? Tomorrow, perhaps? Fanny nodded. That would be good. She pulled back her hood. In the side window, her hair looked like a thicket of nut trees. She got out of the car and stepped straight into a puddle. Karen waved briefly and reversed out onto the road. The beam from her headlights illuminated the winter-wet tree trunks, then she accelerated and the car disappeared behind the woods.

The next day, as Fanny sat on the train home from school, her phone rang. She pulled it out of her pocket and saw that it was an unknown number, so she hesitated a little before answering; she cleared her throat and said hello, with some reticence. It was Karen. She wondered if Fanny would like to go for a walk in the forest. Karen had gone for a long walk herself earlier and discovered a badger's den up on the hillside. She was sure there was a badger there, because she had heard snoring. It sounded the same as when a person breathes heavily in their sleep. Fanny didn't answer immediately, not because she was uncertain, but because she suddenly found the invitation difficult. She ran a finger over her lips. Once in her early teens, she had been determined to join a convent. What an odd thing to remember now! Her mother had wondered: why on earth did Fanny want to go to a nunnery when she was so beautiful? But Fanny was adamant and would not be swayed. That was the good thing about being in a convent, Fanny argued, you could be beautiful there without any consequences.

Karen asked again if Fanny would like to go for a walk. Yes, Fanny would, she said, yes, yes, she wanted to go for a walk.

The train sped past some farmland. A solitary man was walking along the edge of the forest at the end of a muddy field. He trudged back and forth. What was he doing? Was he looking for something? Fanny watched the hunched figure until the train swung round a residential area on the hillside and the man disappeared from view as suddenly as he had appeared.

Karen reversed into the yard. The red brake lights burned bright for a moment in the mist and monochrome. Fanny was standing by the window. As soon as she saw her friend, she thought of Janos. It happened so naturally that at first she didn't notice anything, except that a very ordinary picture of her classmate popped into her head. She was annoyed that this image of him came up. Why should she feel guilty? Why wouldn't he let her go? She knew it was an unreasonable thought. Janos was clearly not holding on to her. She balled her fist and thumped her chest. And was immediately filled by a peculiar peace.

Karen waited by the car. She looked so fragile out there in the grey weather, Fanny thought. It was as though she were standing listening to an imagined echo.

They followed a muddy tractor-tire track into the forest.

The car bounced and twisted over the potholes. Fanny's head banged against the handle above the passenger door a couple of times. Despite the fact that it actually hurt quite a lot, she couldn't help laughing. Karen apologized. It was impossible to avoid the holes. After driving for fifteen minutes, they were so high up that there was snow on the ground, and they could look down over the valley and the patchwork of fields and forest. Then they went down again, past a pine forest. Fanny had always liked the straight, reddish-brown trunks. Freezing rain started to fall.

They stopped by a clearing where there had been logging. The air smelled of resin and damp, stripped bark. They put on the rain boots and stiff, thick work gloves that Karen had brought for them both. Then they followed a path through the trees. It didn't take long before they came to a slope where several of the trees had fallen down. The forest floor was slippery. They had to hold each other up as best they could. Fanny couldn't understand how Karen had managed to walk here before, on her own. She seemed so determined. But had she really come here by accident? Had she parked the car and then, on a whim, chosen this path, through this rugged terrain?

The badger's den was in a stony hollow. Karen led the way down the slope, stopped and froze, put a finger to her lips. It was here, in one of the crevices, that she was sure she had heard the badger. Fanny had never seen a badger before. She crouched down and stared keenly at all the holes and cracks. The two women moved around as quietly as they could, so they might hear or catch a glimpse of the animal, but there were noises everywhere: rustling and trickling, ringing and faint birdsong. Fanny knew that badgers were irascible, but she felt excited as she crept back and forth between the stones, despite the possible danger. After a while, Karen waved Fanny over. They hunkered down and Karen pointed to a narrow passage that was half-hidden by an upturned root. And there it was, loud and clear: breathing. The badger really did sound like a person, and breathed in the same rhythm. Fanny was delighted that they had managed to find the animal. She wanted to put her face as close as possible to the hole, but Karen held her back. There was no need to take unnecessary risks. Even though the creature was clearly asleep, this sleep was probably as light as a veil. They sat there, side by side, whispered to each other as though they had a common language, a single stream of thought. Every now and then the badger grunted, and Karen and Fanny fell into a tense silence. Karen told her that a badger could give a mean bite. They got a hold and then locked their jaws until the bones crunched. Fanny lay down on her stomach and tried to see the animal in the dark. As she lay in this uncomfortable, unnatural position, she felt her heart beating. A beetle crawled over her hand. It was big and black, with a bluish sheen. She swore and shook it off, then flicked it so it flew forward and landed on its back, with its legs waving in the air. Karen lay down beside Fanny. They both kept the palms of their hands to the ground, ready to jump up and run away. The sound from inside the den was so strange, like a steady, whimpering complaint. Karen suspected that the animal had been out hunting all night. There was a smell of carrion by the opening, a sweet stench that came and went on the wind. Karen asked if Fanny thought that animals could dream. As she didn't have any real opinion, Fanny shook her head. The badger was breathing like the haunted, she thought. Karen looked at her blankly. And Fanny dutifully whispered that perhaps animals did see things in a kind of dream or vision. Many animals possessed instincts that meant they were able to register movements in their surroundings through image, even though they were asleep. She heard how forced this interpretation sounded, and so stopped herself by saying that she had no idea, then she got up, stretched her body, and took a few short hops from one stone to the next, away from the opening. Karen followed her. Without turning, Fanny carried on up the slope with the fallen trees. It was dark now, and the forest floor gave way. It was a huge struggle to get back up. Soon Karen's torch swept the ground in front of them, which made things easier. Fanny regretted that she had spoken so freely about something she obviously knew nothing about. If animals had dreams? What did she know about that? She had absolutely no desire to be burdened with uncertain, borrowed opinions.

When they got back up to the trees, Fanny grabbed hold of Karen and apologized. Karen didn't understand. She held the flashlight so the beam shone on Fanny's stomach. What did Fanny mean? Apologize for what? It was as though Karen realized that Fanny had no armour. Fanny shook her head. Nothing. Just a misunderstanding. And the moment of intimacy, this confession that held no reproach, established a kind of finely tuned affection between them, and Fanny found this affection soothing as they walked through the pine forest.

But no sooner were they back at the car than everything turned upside down, and Fanny felt nothing but doubt and conflict inside. And when she got home and was alone again, when she was in the bathroom getting ready for bed, with toothpaste foaming down over her chin, it felt, more than ever, as though no one had any attachment to her.

THE JOY OF
SEEING A
NAIL AGAIN

Fanny wandered around the schoolyard on her own, and chewed on a piece of wood, a bit of a branch from one of the birch trees. She spat, chewed some more, spat. The bell rang and at exactly the same moment, as though orchestrated, a jackhammer started up in one of the side streets. She spotted Janos over by the fountain, which had been closed for winter. He was standing with a couple of girls from one of the other classes. He appeared to be in an excellent mood and was gesticulating wildly. Fanny had not seen him like that before. And when she passed him on her way into the classroom, she overheard that he was talking about particular mountain formations. Mountain formations? Why was he talking about mountain formations? And why were the two girls so interested? When the door closed behind her, Fanny hesitated for a moment. She stood there in the middle of the busy corridor and was not at all perturbed by the looks people gave her. When she regained control, she walked calmly into the classroom and found her place by the window. Not long after, Janos plumped down at his desk in front of her. He typed something into his phone before returning it to the back pocket of his pants. Was it a text message to one of the girls? A suggestion about where to meet? A flirtatious sentence sent in haste? The sound of birds twittering rippled out from the frosty trees that surrounded the schoolyard outside, but there was no comfort in the presence of such indifferent creatures.

On the train, Fanny couldn't find the nail. She searched all the pockets on her coat, without luck. Was there a hole somewhere, so the nail had fallen through into the lining? Fanny stood up and felt in all her pants pockets. And she couldn't find it at home either. She even looked under the sheet, turned the pillowcases inside out, and looked under the bed with a flashlight. Just to be sure. Without joy. The nail had disappeared. She sat down on the edge of the bed. She wanted to cry. She wanted to cry the same inconsolable tears she had cried when she tried unsuccessfully to stop her mother from leaving. It was long after the accident, and it was in a dream. But she didn't cry. No sound passed her lips. She felt ashamed of losing her equilibrium so easily. It was a paradoxical feeling—as though she'd abused her own trust. Because she really was taken aback. And the nonsense with the nail had demanded more self-mastery than she was capable of.

She went out into the garden. It was snowing. She opened her mouth and closed her eyes. And yet it was spring that she imagined. The shimmering birch leaves. Everything was fragrant: jasmine, bird cherry, lilac. It was hard to breathe. Hard to hold your breath. She wasn't sure what was what. She imagined that she looked like a scorched young birch in the midst of all the exuberant growth. But she didn't recognize herself in this image. It was like saying Rome was no longer in Rome. Either she must perish or become a plant that lived without moving, absolutely immovable, deep in the forest. But no, she didn't need to turn her mind inside out to discover that she didn't want to be a passive plant. She was in possession of something else, something changeable, perhaps even mad. She carried an entire war inside her. She stood there, thin in the snow, holding a banal battle that was bigger than herself: a shapeless mass, an irreconcilable face, an unruly fraction among the numbers of the living. But what should she grapple with in order to find peace? What could she think about? Something that didn't make her insecurity too obvious? She was fully aware that there was no such thing as a safe harbour. She wished she could retain a detailed imprint of all the good times, wished she could remember them. But she couldn't recall any clear, happy memories, and any attempt to free herself from confusion and anxiety only resulted in further defeat. She pushed back her hair. It was wet and heavy with snow.

How annoying she could be. She found herself exasperating, unbearable at times. But how could she avoid it? The greater part of what filled her was shaped in the shadows, it was as though what she thought and felt and dreamed acquired new meaning because it was kept secret, yet everything kept hidden and anonymous was important only to her. She often tried to find meaning in all kinds of everyday things. She could trudge without purpose over a field on a frosty November morning and think to herself that all the decapitated straws that had been left behind held their own inscrutable mysteries, had their own mission, just as much as the precious heads that had been sent away for refinement had theirs. But what good was it if things kept their meaning hidden within their own limited life? Loneliness had no advantages. Loneliness did not have the same weight or value as independence or integrity. More than anything, loneliness was hopelessness and privation. Everything Fanny thought and felt went unnoticed: the snowflakes floating down couldn't care less about anything at all. And because she wanted to believe that was the case, that was what she believed. The damp cold flushed out a sudden cough. She doubled up and spat. In the silence that followed, she heard the almost imperceptible sound of a car engine, then a car door closing and the crunching of feet on the frozen dirt. It was Alm. He smiled, but his face remained serious. Without a word, he gave Fanny a hug. His stubble scraped her cheek.

He stood in front of her mute, still wearing a crooked smile, as though he was trying to make amends for some inadequacy or another. The moon withdrew behind an abundance of clouds. And finally, in the unilluminated space between them, Alm asked if Fanny would like to go for a drive. Bewildered by this odd and late request, Fanny could not bring herself to say no. She had to be up early the next morning, but of course she could go for a drive.

They headed toward town. Despite the fact that it was late, the traffic was intense and ablaze, like blood circulation gone wild. Alm had put on some music: Mozart, it said on the CD player, and then there was a long, informative title that Fanny read several times, as though it was a riddle she had to solve: "Wolfgang Amadeus Mozart—Sinfonia concertante for violin and viola, E-flat major, K. 364. Allegro maestoso."

It was sleeting heavily now, and they both sat in silence behind the wet windshield. The freezing rain was like a pushy person. It wanted something: it wanted them to start talking, it was important that they speak. But the music filled the car so bewitchingly. It was impossible to interrupt, impossible to cut it off. With what? Fanny had nothing on her mind. She had been reluctant but polite regarding the drive. She had understood that Alm had something on his mind. That he wanted to talk, tell her something important. Was he ill? Was he dying? Terminal stomach cancer? Was this goodbye?

In the middle of a bridge, Alm swung to the side without warning. The traffic whizzed by, and someone hit their horn in anger. Fanny could see the town lights through the gaps in the guardrail, shining and flickering like a lab bench full of colourful bottles. Alm apologized for the sudden and dangerous manoeuvre. He had forgotten something. It was embarrassing. And completely absurd to seek out Fanny so late. He hoped she would forgive him. Could she? A freight train passed under the bridge below them, making it impossible for Fanny to answer. There was nothing to forgive. She wouldn't mind an explanation, but Alm would have to volunteer that. She wanted to go home. She was tired. Tired of Alm as well, but that would pass, if only she got some sleep.

The minister dropped Fanny on the road, lifted his hand in farewell, and drove on. Fanny had forgotten to lock the door. She went in and went to bed in the dark. Fortunately her doubts were not strong enough to last. She fell asleep almost immediately and dreamed of nothing.

The next day, in the unpredictable weather, on her way to school, she thought that no matter what Alm had wanted to tell her, she was glad he had not offered up any confessions or farewell speeches. She sat at her desk and tried to follow the class. Janos had not shown up. It was more a relief than that she missed him. The biology teacher was talking about micro-organisms. Fanny couldn't take it all in. She only caught the odd word or phrase: "independent life forms," "saline concentration," "rotifers," "yeast extracts," and "mite." She thought about the music Alm had played in the car the evening before: Mozart, she remembered, and a concept she hadn't understood: allegro maestoso. In secret, with almost imperceptible lip movements, she tried to remember the melody, to hum without a sound. She soon gave up. She tipped back her chair. Something clattered on the floor. She must have hit something with the chair leg. A soft noise as the teacher went on and on. She leaned forward, bent down, ran her fingertips over the floor. And there was the nail. It was shiny and sharp. She picked it up and slipped it carefully, almost like a thief, into her back pocket.

A SAD ENDING
IN THE MIDDLE
OF A STORY

Fanny stood on the overcrowded platform and waited for a train it seemed would never come. An announcement had been made that all departures would be delayed by fifteen to twenty minutes, apparently due to a power outage in one of the tunnels, but more than thirty minutes had now passed, and there were no new announcements.

On the opposite platform, on the other side of the double tracks, a man was standing in front of an advertisement of a smiling woman's face, and he kept glancing over at her. He was quite an attractive man, Fanny thought. Tall and thin, a bit gangly like herself. Around thirty, maybe a bit older. She'd noticed him there in among all the people. And now they stood looking at each other from their respective islands, without any attempt to disguise it, like a flame flickering yellow in the biting wind. A single freight engine emerged from one of the depots. It chugged by with an insistent whine that managed to cut through deep throbbing. Was it driverless? It appeared to be. And when it had passed, Fanny could no longer see the man she had been flirting with. She looked up and down the platform, but he was no longer there. She flapped her arms to keep warm. An elderly couple emerged from the tunnel that ran under the tracks. They pushed their way through the crowds to stand in front of Fanny. The woman was enveloped in a cloud of sweet perfume. In loud voices, they squabbled and complained about the delay. Fanny found herself repulsed by the quarrelsome pair, but then regretted having such hostile feelings. The resistance she felt was a complex calculation that would eventually equal zero. Then all of a sudden there was someone else standing next to her. A man's voice whispered in her ear. Where was she going? She turned around. It was the man from the platform opposite. He smelled of winter grass. That was the first thing she noticed and she said it straight out, without thinking, that he smelled of grass. He looked at her, astonished. Was that a good thing? She nodded. She shivered. Her teeth were chattering. The man asked if she would like a cup of coffee—after all, there were no trains. Fanny nodded again, nodded a bit too quickly, she thought, she should have given it a few seconds, a slight hesitation, but what was done was done, he could think what he liked, that she was easy prey, perhaps it was true, perhaps she was a poor desperate girl. But he would see that she had integrity all the same. This was not a foolish surrender to any old passing promise of love or short-lived intimacy. He would soon realize that.

They found a shabby and almost deserted café right by the station. The weather was not conducive to wandering around looking for a better place. Only once they were inside with the smell of fresh baking did they introduce themselves: he was called Fredrik. They ordered two coffees and sat down at one of the tables by the window. Would Fanny like anything to eat? No, thank you. The café looked out over an empty square that was dignified by two big, shining silver sculptures: enormous, abstract shapes that twisted and rippled up to meet the falling wet snow. Did Fanny like the sculptures? Fanny didn't answer. She was focused on drinking the scalding coffee without burning her mouth. Fredrik talked while Fanny sipped the hot liquid, blew on it, and sipped again. She mustn't think this was something he did every day, he stressed. But she had looked so beautiful standing there. He couldn't just let it go, leave without making some kind of contact. Then he would have thought about her for the rest of his life—the beautiful girl at the train station. Outside, the snow melted into a heavy downpour, fast hard rain. The sky above the square took on a greyish sheen. Fanny finished her coffee and put her cup down. It banged on the saucer. What was she going to say? What was she going to give back? Of all things, she said that she didn't have a boyfriend, that she was free. She regretted it. She simply meant that she too had felt a connection. And thought that it would be sad if he just disappeared. Fredrik took hold of her hand over the table. He was careful, hesitant, he took her hands in his, which were as big as a carpenter's. Fanny thought about Karen. Karen had such graceful hands, long fingers. This Fredrik had strong, rough fingers. He turned one of her hands over, and Fanny saw that he immediately noticed the scratches on her wrist. She pulled her hand from his grasp and covered herself by pulling down the sleeve of her sweater, and in a nonchalant but natural movement, she lifted her coffee cup again, even though it was empty, apart from the grounds, and took a sip, or a pretend sip. She chewed on the grounds. They tasted bitter. She wanted him to say something. She wanted him to say anything at all just to show that he was not concerned about her accident. She wanted him to believe that it was an accident, that she had brushed against a piece of knotted wood or fallen in some thorny undergrowth. They sat looking at each other in a sudden glow of light that confused Fanny. It burst through a crack in the clouds, in through the café window, and shone on her for a brief moment. She felt she was almost transparent. It was unbearable. He apologized and then said again how beautiful she was. Fanny shook her head. She stood up. Should they go? She was about to ask where they should go, but didn't.

They went to the station. The trains were running again. If Fanny hurried, she could catch hers. She didn't know what to do. She waited. She waited for him to make a decision. He stroked her cheek, said they could meet another time. Fanny had hoped for something else, something more. She hid her disappointment by saying okay. She had hoped he would take her with him, he would take her somewhere, she wouldn't have to wait, wouldn't have to wonder if he wanted her. Was it the wounds on her wrist that had put him off? She thought, uncertain of how deep the thought went, that it was probably easier to accept love when it was wrung out of its true form.

IT'S NICE HERE, ISN'T IT?

For the last, deserted stretch of the journey, Fanny was the only person on the bus. It was just her and the driver, a man she couldn't remember having seen before. A dark figure at the front of the bus, partially hidden by the smoked glass partition. Hands on the wheel. Impatient? The otherwise familiar land-scape felt unknown, not because it was distorted or changed, there was only the slightest difference, but all the same—a careful transformation that disturbed and confused Fanny. The half-light on the bus was filled with dust, dust or spores that floated and flared up in the irregular light from passing cars. A transport truck thundered by, a whine and a reverberating flash, cold as a blade. And in the same instant, Fanny felt something take hold of her. Something invisible and inaudible lifted her up from where she sat. She grabbed the back of the seat to keep herself grounded, so she wouldn't bounce against the roof. But then she let go all the same, pulled back her hand. It was pure reflex, as though she'd unexpectedly touched a hot burner. In a slow, circular, and completely uncontrollable movement she rose into the air. And through the small hatch in the roof—or was it plastic?—through the transparent square she saw the wide-open night sky. She stretched up, squashed her face against the pane. There was the Milky Way, that glittering and bubbling cluster was the Milky Way. She was floating. She was hovering. She didn't make a sound, but she thought her voice would carry in space. Her voice, even the slightest sound from a living being would be a welcome solution. A solution to what? Fanny didn't know. She was filled with goodwill and compassion, as people so often are in the face of torment and loss. It was like being picked up by a welcome wind. A wind that blew until morning, when once again everything around her was definable and concrete: the bedside lamp, hair band, waterglass—solid, material, all of it.

Fanny got out of bed and stood in front of the full-length mirror that leaned against the wall. She looked at her thin body. Behind the shiny surface she was someone else. In there she was a child, a little girl, and her face was luminous. The little girl lifted her hand and wanted to touch her forehead, but then Fanny turned away and went over to the window. Outside the window, she saw the crown of a tree blowing and shimmering, and the light was like a fairy tale: three suns, the bluest sky, and the greenest grass. Outside the window, in the early dawn, in the late dusk, the clouds moved like dark stains on Japanese rice paper. Fanny was in the world, she existed there. And the little girl existed in the mirror behind her. But "existed" in what sense?

BUT ONE OF
THE CALENDER
WINDOWS
WAS EMPTY

(...)

AS THOUGH
FAVOURED
BY FATE

It felt like she was demanding an explanation, a clarification, as soon as she entered the church. She stamped the snow off her shoes and took a few steps down the aisle. She stopped and stroked the water from her hair. She clenched her hands, folded them, wiped a drop of melted snow from her knee. Her sweater smelled of cold earth. Bloody miserable weather. She called for Alm, albeit not too loudly, but got no answer. And there was no one in the vestry. She gave the bench a light kick. Why was it that even in carefree moments she was aware of life passing, that life was running out, that she was dragging a skeleton around with her, a death mask under her skin? And if she by chance should find peace, were God or Fate or Providence worried that she might go half mad with gratitude? Be unable to master a trouble-free existence, unable to cope with being in balance, at rest? She sat down on the same bench she had just kicked in irritation. She stretched her arms out to the side, leaned her head back, and laughed a little at herself—the laughter was so unforeseen. It must have been the pale light that made everything seem so bleak. But now, quite unexpectedly, a sense of fun blew through her, and it was almost unseemly. She remembered that a badger's den often had three entrances, or perhaps it would be more correct to say three exits, three escapes, three possibilities.

Alm came into the church carrying a huge, dusty candle holder, the kind used during Advent that stands on the floor with big pillar candles firmly fixed on spikes. It looked heavy, as it was made from wrought iron that sung out when Alm put it down by the altar. Despite the fact that he had come in from the cold, he was wearing thin clothes and his sleeves were rolled up. Fanny wanted to help, but Alm waved her away. He said nothing about their absurd meeting. He seemed to be fretting. It was as if something had robbed him of his energy. He had been carrying the wrought-iron candle holder as a tired labourer might carry a stone at the end of the day. The task had been anything but pleasurable. He seemed to enjoy nothing, not even without thinking, in the way that hands holding an apple enjoy the sensation. Was a feeling of guilt holding him back? Once again, Fanny had to smile at her imagination running wild. She was fantasizing and making things up, and ultimately it was all due to her own confusion, deep down. To help him, she started to pick the hard wax off the huge candle holder. Alm handed her a penknife. Fanny took it. She opened out the solid blade and carried on with the laborious work.

Fanny was not one to speculate if other people's lives were like this or that. In the same way that she kept her memory in check, she was only interested in what happened after she had met someone. She was only concerned about what they shared, the rest didn't matter. But now she wanted to know more, she put aside this extreme discretion and asked Alm straight out to tell her about himself. Alm scratched his cheek, rasped his stubble. He ran a hand over the crown of his head. What should he tell her? Something from his childhood? Fanny shrugged. Anything, whatever popped into his head. They sat down on a pew, and Alm started to talk, hesitant at first, but not reluctant. Once when he was a boy, not much older than five, he had woken up in the middle of the night. It was late summer. They lived in a big house by a lake, his parents, him, and two older sisters, twins. He often woke up in the middle of the night, especially in summer when the air was heavy, and then he got up and wandered around the slumbering house, drunk with sleep and without a plan, like a lost down-and-outer. The lights were on in the living room. Someone had forgotten to turn them off. His sisters, no doubt, who often sat up late with a board game after the others had gone to bed. The glass door that led out to the garden was wide open and a draft lifted the light curtains so they billowed and fanned the light out over the slate steps and lawn. Then he noticed the quick, shifting shadows fluttering around the ceiling rose. A bat had got in through the open door. It dived and flew in desperate circles. It made furious noises, grazed his head. He stood there terrified and screamed, woke the whole house. His father and mother and sisters came running from the bedrooms upstairs. There was quite a commotion in the night-silent house. His father immediately ordered them to turn off the lights, and to light a candle and put it in the doorway to the garden. He said the flame would lure the rascal out of the room and out of the house.

Then the story was finished. There was no more. Alm stood up. Fanny wanted to know if it had worked, if the bat flew out. Alm told her that it had. But Fanny should read books, he said. Fanny should read instead of listening to the tales of old chatterboxes. Did they not read at school anymore? The minister disappeared into the vestry, came back with a book. It was for Fanny. Had she read the book he gave her last time? Had she read about Mouchette? No, Fanny had not read it. She didn't say it out loud, but she suspected that reading was perhaps not for her. It felt like a duty, a burden. And what was more, she couldn't concentrate, always found herself sitting there staring at the same page, at the jumble of words and letters, for an eternity, with no result other than exhaustion and frustration over her lack of discipline. Perhaps accepting Alm's gift would crystallize her determination, the determination to read at least one page every evening. She accepted it. Wolfgang Hildesheimer, it said on the white title page, and under the author's name: Tynset. Tynset? Fanny looked up at Alm, as though the title required some explanation. She opened the book and read the first few sentences in a quiet voice: "I am lying in bed, in my winter bed. It is time to sleep. But when is it not?" Then she turned to a random page further on in the book: "Tynset—it sounds a bit like Hamlet, does it not? Yes, it sounds like Hamlet, strange that I have only thought of that now." Alm held out his hand. Fanny stood up and took it. Could she promise to read the two books he had given her? She didn't hesitate this time. She answered immediately. She promised to read both books. Alm's grip was firm, and he didn't let go until she had given him her promise. Goodbyes are embarrassing, he said, if not downright pointless.

DREAMED
MUSIC

Fanny liked to go for walks along the railway line. She liked to feel the air pressure from the passing trains. And it felt wonderful to wander along the tracks like this with Karen. It was the first Sunday of Advent. Karen had woken her up. She had already rung several times before Fanny, who had her cellphone on silent, saw the display light up on the bedside table. Fanny had lain in bed and read Wolfgang Hildesheimer's novel until late in the night, and she had been so tired that she had to read several of the paragraphs a number of times before she understood what was going on, and, fascinated by what she experienced, she struggled on as best she could before the reading eventually lost out to sleep.

They had left the car in the clearing where the skiers normally park. It had been sleeting for a few days, but nothing had settled, and the tracks that had been prepared were largely spoiled. There was no one out in the rotten tracks, due to the lack of snow. Fanny walked a few steps behind Karen. They went through an old underpass to get to the other side of the railway line. It smelled of mud inside the rust-coloured tunnel. They stopped at the entrance and shouted as loud as they could, but it was too short, little more than five or six metres long, so there was no echo. Karen wanted to know what Fanny had been up to since they last met. Fanny didn't know what to say. She didn't want to tell her about the man she had met. The whole thing was a fiasco. And what did Karen care that Fanny had been to the church and scraped wax off a wrought-iron candle holder? But she was reading a book. So, when the two women were still in the tunnel, Fanny told her with great enthusiasm that she had started to read a book. It was like cutting a watermelon, first one had to get the blade through the stubborn rind, it took time and effort, but then it sliced easily through the flesh and the juice and pips ran out. She was in the middle of a book by a German author called Wolfgang Hildesheimer. And this Wolfgang Hildesheimer had written about a tiny place in Norway, a place where he had never been. The book was about a man in Germany who dreamed and fantasized about this small place in Norway, the mountain municipality of Tynset. The man, who was the protagonist of the book, had come across a road map of Norway quite by accident, and thus discovered an insignificant place called Tynset. It lay in the north of Østerdal, on the Røros line – and he, that is to say the protagonist in Wolfgang Hildesheimer's novel, noticed the name "Tynset", because he thought it resembled "Hamlet". Karen wanted to know if he ever went to Tynset, but no, Wolfgang Hildesheimer never visited Tynset. And the protagonist—it even said on the cover of the book—the protagonist, whose name Fanny had forgotten, never went to Tynset either.

They carried on for a few hundred metres along the tracks before turning down a slope that led to a stream. A loud freight train whizzed by, and even though they were some way from the tracks, they could feel the air pressure. The sucking pull made them stop, and with their hands to their ears, they watched the line of wagons pass. Only now, when they were standing like this, like two frightened children, did Fanny wonder where they were going. Without asking Karen where or why, she had said yes to going for a walk. Karen had no better answer than that she wanted to go for a walk, and she felt like company.

She liked the uneven terrain, liked climbing, liked tramping through scrubs and thickets, especially on a grey winter's day.

They came to a clearing in the forest. The only sound they could hear was the distant hum of the motorway that cut through the valley to the east. Karen stopped and stood still, with her back to Fanny. Was she listening to something? Something other than the traffic? Without anything being said, Fanny knew immediately that she should not disturb her. What was happening? What was she witnessing? Karen didn't move, stood as though petrified. The soles of her boots sank down into the cold, damp forest floor. The grass and plants glittered with frost, the drops of water on the moss had frozen. Without twisting her body, Karen turned her head toward Fanny, it was a strange and awkward movement. She lifted her finger to her lips, whispered hush, and asked: Can you hear the music? Fanny could not hear any music. Did Karen mean the cars in the distance? No, it was music. Could Fanny really not hear that it was music? Fanny shook her head. She heard only the cars and the odd pigeon. Karen got out her cellphone. She had an app that could recognize pieces of music. Because it was definitely music, no doubt about it. It was just strange that Fanny couldn't hear it. Karen held her phone up in the air. Fanny listened to nothing. About a minute passed, then Karen held out the phone toward her, so she could read what it said on the screen: "Wolfgang Amadeus Mozart—Sinfonia concertante for violin and viola, E-flat major, K. 364. Allegro maestoso." Fanny strained her ears to pick up the sound, the music, but where she was standing, there was no music to be heard, no tune or notes to lose oneself in. It was getting dark, and shadows fell across the clearing. It happened quickly. It was as though the whole forest twisted in the sunset. The shadows of the trees ran past them like living creatures in flight.

When Fanny woke up, she was calm. She was lying on her

stomach in bed. It was an unfamiliar but not uncomfortable position. She stretched her arm out from under the duvet and saw the thin scratches on her skin. They were so precise. It was almost comical. Fanny thought they looked like a code. A code for something worthless. She turned over onto her back and pulled the duvet up under her chin. She had not cried, and there was an odd sense of relief in the irrationality of it—not bursting into tears. But equally, she was open to the idea that something, whatever it might be, could give expression to this loss. But the loss was a lack, and she could not get beyond that lack. Should she let her memories in? But opening up and letting the memories in, the images and events flow by—no, what was the point of that?

FANNY

REMEMBERED

Karen persuaded Fanny to go to the disco in town. A club in one of the back streets that ran from the square to the train station. Fanny felt giddy and elated as soon as she and her friend entered the packed venue. Everything around them was glowing. The faces in the red-and-blue light, the sparkling haze between the dreamlike figures, the deep, pulsing music. What did they all hope to find? What was Fanny looking for herself, as she moved, wide-eyed, through the throng? It wasn't acknowledgement. Or the fabulous gift of happiness. Perhaps it was something as simple as blinding validation in the midst of all the jostling.

After a few rounds of a bitter, orange drink at the bar, which Karen recommended and paid for, the two women went out onto the dance floor. More and more new bodies pressed between them in the crowd. Faces appeared and disappeared one after the other. Fanny enjoyed the movements, enjoyed her own lightness. And the alcohol was already taking effect. She felt that her thoughts were clearer than ever. It was like being liberated from a vague sense of self-sacrifice, no, not sacrifice, nothing quite so honourable. Thanks to a self-inflicted misunderstanding, she had simply attached herself to a tragic absence. And now she allowed herself to be filled with a sense of profound pleasure. She saw herself in another light and there was something heartfelt and justified about what she saw. She put an arm round Karen's waist. She remembered her parents. The small family. That they had played hide-and-seek with Margit from the neighbouring farm, and the two girls had hidden up in the loft. In their enthusiasm, or driven by the wildest fantasies, they had pulled old clothes out from a chest: a raincoat, boots, some colourful shawls, and a dusty woollen sweater. When they were recovering from all the excitement with an evening snack, they were both struck down with a sudden fever, and at bedtime, when they brushed their teeth, they stood together for about half an hour and studied their faces and posture in the mirror. Fanny wanted to tell Karen about it, but she froze whenever she remembered things from her childhood, so she just kept quiet.

While Karen danced with another woman, Fanny stood at the bar with yet another of the colourful drinks. She was starting to feel a little woozy, but was clear enough to realize she was jealous. It was a shameful feeling. She didn't want to be someone who was mean and anxious like that. And what was it that she and Karen had anyway? A friendship? No other ties. No promises. Or were they lovers? There was nothing Fanny wanted more. It was as though they had approached each other in measured movements. But now, and it was very confusing, they were tied to each other in such a way that every word they spoke was a confirmation. Fanny put down the empty glass and leaned her elbows on the bar. She watched the two women. She had a notion to send Karen a text message, a message that would arrive unheard as she danced. Fanny tapped it quickly into her phone: "It was you who invited me and I gladly said yes to your generosity." She sent the message without hesitating, but as soon as it had gone, she regretted it, because what good would a message like that do? She could just as well have gone over to her friend and whispered in her ear that from now on she would surrender herself completely. Was she really jealous? Was that what it was? She didn't want to admit it, she wanted to steer clear of having to admit it, even to herself. But all these loose thoughts were stripped of any meaning when a man with a shaved head lurched toward Fanny and spilled beer all over her. The drink splashed softly on her neck and shoulders. Fanny grabbed hold of him, not to shout at him, but to help him stay on his feet. A bouncer appeared. He took care of the drunkard and showed Fanny the way to the restroom by jerking his thumb toward a narrow corridor at the back of the club.

The restroom was full of people as well. Once she had finally managed to press her way forward to one of the sinks, Fanny took off her jacket and top. She stood there, her upper body bare, and let the cold water run over her clothes. The sickening smell of malt was soon rinsed away. A red-haired woman with silver glitter sprinkled on her cheeks leaned toward her. Fanny didn't catch what she said. The woman pointed at Fanny's wrist and mumbled something inaudible. Fanny wanted to pull on the soaking wet top, but it wouldn't cooperate, it twisted and rolled up over her back. The woman with the glitter didn't seem bothered by the awkward situation. She draped her arms invitingly over Fanny's shoulders and wanted to dance. Fanny managed to pull her top down over her stomach, grabbed her jacket, and tried to get free. The woman put her mouth to Fanny's ear, and now she could hear what she was saying—two straightforward sentences: she shouldn't cut herself, she was so beautiful. And why wouldn't she dance? Fanny pulled herself loose and pushed her way out. Karen was nowhere to be seen. Fanny thought that perhaps she had misunderstood. They had not gone to the club as a couple, as lovers. They were just friends. And to be fair—nothing had been said. No promises. No assurances. One didn't get very far like that. But if everything had to be said, if everything had to be unambiguous in order to be seen as a deal, as an honest touch, what should she believe then? What should she make of the day they spent in the forest, the badger's den and the kiss, all the friendliness? And the undeniable attraction—was that not the bond itself? Was that not the basis of their relationship?

Fanny went home without saying anything. It was a long and arduous journey. The last train had long since gone, and the only alternative was the night bus. Fanny didn't get home until nearly four in the morning. Before going to bed, she checked her phone. Karen had tried to ring her several times. Only now did it dawn on Fanny that there was of course an uncomplicated and reasonable explanation. She hadn't exactly looked for her friend in the flickering dark. She was angry with herself for having reacted in such a rash and infantile way. She put her hands to her face in irritation. She wanted so badly to whisper something to Karen, an apology if nothing else. But what would Karen say? Some comforting words perhaps. Or simply that she already found Fanny's choices bizarre. Fanny thought: if I'm going to be me, if I'm going to be me all my life…I can't bear it.

BARELY
TWENTY-FOUR
HOURS HAD
PASSED BEFORE
SHE FOUND
HERSELF IN
THE FUTURE

Karen was standing waiting outside the school gates in the drifting snow. They hugged briefly, both equally reserved, as if it was required of them. Fanny presumed that Karen wanted to ask what had happened to her the night before, but no questions were asked. Instead, Karen told her that she'd never really liked Plato, his philosophy, which basically made the whole world an illusion. Fanny said they had not really touched on Plato at school. After all, she was still only in high school. Karen had hated high school. She had barely scraped through. It just dragged on and on. You have no idea what it was like, she said. But Fanny did have an idea. Fanny knew only too well what Karen was talking about. Karen didn't have much time for Aristotle either. He thought he knew everything. He really believed he had a full overview—simply because he was able to divide things up into categories. And Socrates—well, it was as though no one had had any ideas before him.

The two women crossed the street together. Fanny was at a loss: why was Karen talking about these philosophers who she must have known were no more than distant figures, shadows almost, in Fanny's world?

They found a bakery in the busy, Christmas-decorated pedestrian street. There was an odd stiffness between them, but fortunately Karen managed to change the mood. When they had each been given their coffee at a table by the window, she commented on Fanny's miserable face. She said it looked like someone had died. And surely Fanny realized that all her talk about philosophers was just nonsense. An explanation would not only be welcome, she continued, it was wanted. She blew on her coffee, then put it down without drinking. Fanny realized that this was the obvious part of what they shared: whatever it was that was unspoken, and yet understood, the simplicity of Karen's messages. Fanny reached over the table, the ends of her scarf dipped in her coffee, and like an insistent fortune teller, she laid her trembling hand on Karen's brow. Strangely enough, she liked it when Karen was pleased with herself, and Karen seemed to be pleased with herself right now. Fanny thought she was like Janos. They were both screwed together in such a way that they seemed to be interested in absolutely everything the world had to offer, and what they thought about everything was also of great importance. Fanny said: You're a very religious person, only you don't believe in a god. Or is it the other way around? Karen put her hand round Fanny's wrist. What did Fanny know about what she did or didn't believe? Karen kissed the palm of her hand, pushed it away, and drank her coffee. She took her time, as though mulling over what had been said, what it actually meant.

Fanny felt a bit desperate when Karen asked about her plans for Christmas. To answer that she had no idea what she was going to do might seem invasive, a bit dejected, so she told the truth and said that for the past couple of years she'd taken it easy over Christmas. She'd watched old films on television, made meals that were befitting of a celebration, slept more than usual, and enjoyed living a life of leisure for a few days. Karen stared out the window. It was getting dark already. The lights in town were on night and day. Christmas decorations twinkled. Karen seemed to realize that this was an opportunity to be grabbed, because she stood up, took a few steps toward the door, and waved for Fanny to follow. And Fanny understood what it meant. It struck her: Karen was clearly not a superstitious person, but rather filled with an insatiable curiosity. Fanny found this highly entertaining.

As soon as they were out in the falling snow, someone called to Fanny. It was Janos. He shook hands with them. Fanny introduced Karen. She thought that men were not bothered by silence. But now it was she who was not bothered. She waited. She let the silence grow. And in that way, she forced Janos to say something: where was Fanny off to? Had she finished the work for tomorrow? Wasn't it lovely, the way the snow made everything brighter? Fanny gave friendly answers to all his trivial questions. The meeting lasted only a few minutes, then Janos held out his hand in farewell, this time less emphatically, more by accident, as though distracted, and even though Fanny didn't want to embarrass him, it felt good to see him uncertain for a moment. And it was as if Karen instinctively understood what Fanny was thinking and feeling, and she wasted no time in confirming it. She took Fanny by the arm and they walked across the square together. No questions. The car was parked on one of the side streets by the bus station. Karen offered to drive Fanny home and asked if she had a spare toothbrush.

THERE WAS A
VOICE THAT
SPOKE TO HER,
DAY AND NIGHT,
THAT WAS
NEVER QUIET,
BUT SHE ASSUMED
IT WOULD DIE
WITH HER, OR...

Fanny and Karen sat at the breakfast table. Karen had got up early. She had already boiled a couple of eggs and made toast that smelled of butter. Fanny rubbed her eyes and yawned. She gulped down her coffee, which she had cooled with some milk. She thought, and it was a welcome thought, that after last night she was no longer shy of Karen. Their friendship had started by accident, with a punctured bicycle tire, and they had since become inseparable. Now it seemed so obvious that they would find each other—predetermined. That is what Fanny thought, at least. And later on that morning, after being driven to school, as she sat in the classroom writing down sentences from an essay the class had read as homework, she thought with pleasure about what was to come. In the past couple of years, she had fallen into the habit of feeling anxious whenever she dwelled on things that made her happy, but now it seemed that the bliss, and it wasn't wrong to call it bliss, would not subside. It was as though a prolonged struggle was finally over. And even though this happiness presumably did not have its roots in her, Fanny experienced the newness of it as liberating, a release. So when Janos turned round and asked if he could borrow a pencil sharpener, she answered with no inhibition, almost with abandon, in fact, that of course he could. She opened her pencil case, jabbed herself—it was the nail, but she paid no heed to its reappearance—found the sharpener, and handed it to Janos.

Fanny had not been able to sleep that night, or the night before. And now she found herself in an extension of that sleeplessness. Her thoughts were all like some mysterious, romantic unfolding. She was buoyed by the bright-eyed rhythm of the day. And everything around her carried with it renewal, a sharp, cool clarity.

Her cellphone, set to silent, flashed on the desk in front of her. It was a message from Karen, who wondered if they should meet on Saturday morning. Perhaps they could drive to the coast? Fanny wanted to answer. She touched the screen and noticed only then that her fingertip was bleeding, nothing worth mentioning, that stupid nail, it was just annoying. What had she been thinking? It felt so alien to her now. It kept appearing like Morse code in a prison. It had been her secret ally but now was no more than a mean reminder of who she had been: a person who didn't belong in her own life. When she got home, she dropped her bag and coat in the hall, and went out to the woodshed. She got out a hammer, put the nail to one of the beams, and hammered it deep into the wood. She whispered a question: Can you hear me? She listened for the answer, really listened, but not for long, and without any expectations, because she knew, of course, of course Fanny knew that it was pointless, of course she didn't expect the nail to answer. But by enquiring, by this simple personification, she rid herself of the contradiction that had weighed her down for so long: this ordinary, this innocent but demanding, tool of destruction.

A WHITE PONY

Fanny and Karen drove to the coast. A bitter wind blew here and there, and any water the sea had allowed to wash over the land, then carelessly left behind, was now frozen in waves, pools, and puddles that reflected nothing, that didn't sparkle at all, even though the sky was still lit with its own matte shine. The wind had picked up through the morning. It was not snowing, but any moisture froze. White flakes danced haphazardly in the air, the vegetation that bordered the stretch of sand darkened, and the breakers swelled and threw themselves higher and higher. Karen climbed up onto some rocks and stared out to sea. Fanny pulled up her hood and trudged over the hard-packed sand. A swath of white foam rose up from a breaker and, just before it flattened out, the flapping foam rag looked like a horse, a pony that was desperate to avoid death by drowning. Fanny picked up a stick and threw it at the flailing beast. The pony reared hastily and finally managed to tear itself loose before a gust of wind blew it apart. It was an unusual disappearance. It was as though the dead had fleetingly stepped into the world of the living.

Fanny and Karen wandered along the water's edge. They followed a stretch of coarse sand and red rocks. In some places ice had formed in among the stones and they had to take care. They guided and helped each other over the slippery rock formations. Out on a cliff, Karen stood close to Fanny, put a hand into her hood, and pushed back her hair. It's strange, isn't it?

she said. Isn't it strange how things inherit certain characteristics along with their names? Fanny didn't understand what she meant, but she said yes all the same, it was strange. Where did Fanny get her name from? She had once asked her mother and been told: Ardant, Ardant. Which left Fanny none the wiser.

They walked back to the car and drove home. There was an open bottle of red wine on the kitchen table. They had a glass each and then went into the bathroom to get undressed and ready for bed. They lay down under the same duvet, found one another in something that resembled a familiar embrace, and fell asleep.

THE FARMS
BY THE SEA

The third Sunday in Advent. What did Fanny dream about? What she remembered, what she thought about during the day, what stayed with her through the night: a panic attack on the way to a funeral, pigeons roosting on a branch, a street with faded facades, and rain that blurred in the dimming light. A girl swimming in a lake, an old disintegrated film roll in a metal box.

Fanny wandered around the deserted building looking for someone to post a letter for her. Why she wasn't able to do it herself, and who the letter was to was unclear, the important thing was to get it sent.

When she woke up, she was alone. It was already late in the day, and Karen had presumably not had the heart to wake her before she drove home. There were no tracks, no indication in the snow that blanketed the farm, only windswept surfaces. Fanny got dressed and went down to the living room. She curled up on the sofa with one of the books she had been given by Alm, the story of Mouchette: "Her thin body had given her no grounds for vanity…"

Fanny disappeared into a state of drowsy attention. She was a starving child who had been served a meal. The pages, sentences, images rose up in front of her, inside her, became realities, actual events. And when Mouchette so fervently wanted the bastard Mathieu to die, Fanny wanted him to die too. Mouchette's despair became Fanny's despair. In her innocence, Mouchette thought the murder of a brutal gamekeeper was worse than the rape of a fourteen-year-old girl, and that both crimes were punishable by law, the incomprehensible law that always made the poor pay. Fanny felt so despondent and angry that she had to stop reading. She threw the novel down on the sofa. It bounced off the sofa's arm and landed on the floor with a small thud. So she had to deal with it after all. She picked up the book, put it under her arm, and went out into the kitchen, stirred some chocolate powder into a glass of milk to comfort herself. Why had this day made her so sad? And that all-consuming novel—how could something made-up fill her with such gloom and desperation? And why had Alm given her these two books in particular, handed them to her with such express demands? The one book was about the saddest of lives, the other about not getting to where one wants to be, never arriving at the place of one's dreams, a kind of collapse or journey that's never started. And much more: "lie and stay lying forever and let Tynset disappear—, I see it vanish over there, it is already far away, and now it is gone altogether, the name is forgotten, gone with the wind like an echo and smoke, a final breath—" Yes, that book unsettled her as well.

Fanny stared out the kitchen window as she drank the chocolate milk. The roads were quiet. The houses that were closest seemed deserted and forlorn. Farther away on the horizon lay the big farms, one after the other, along the water's edge, Sunday silent and idle. She spotted a helicopter gliding over the hazy pillars of chimney smoke. The sound of the rotor blades somehow delayed in flight. She missed the summer. The winter had been so long. It felt like it had stretched out over years. It snuffled and shuffled on. The snow and cold were in their prime. The summer belonged to a forgotten time or, at best, imagined. Fanny put her hands to her face, opened her fingers. In the July heat, the air between the wooden slats of the outhouse shimmered. In the July heat, the roof on the woodshed smelled of tarred paper—it was as though all manner of abandon carried with it a friendly echo: a mare neighing in a paddock, road dust that was yellow with pollen, a veneer of something almost sublime cast on everything by the generous light. The winter was well-advanced now. It was the sharp, crackling cold that ruled. The days were short; they hurried by, as erratic as a wounded dog. They weren't like days at all, more like a dull and petulant exchange between dawn and dusk.

Fanny picked up her phone. Should she perhaps call Karen, to say that she missed her? Could she perhaps just say how miserable she felt? No, it would sound stupid. It was important for Fanny to stand on her own two feet, to be independent. Especially in relation to Karen. Dependent? No, she would rather admit something even more embarrassing: that she had struggled to tie her own shoelaces until puberty. Without thinking, she ran her hand over the white scars on her forearm. A curious tremor ran through her body. Perhaps she was cold. Or was it some kind of maternal sympathy that she turned in on herself? Could she stand up? Could she walk? Yes, everything was in perfect working order. So she wasn't ill. She was well. She was healthy. She wasn't mad, or uncritical, or numbed by doubt or conviction. She had a life, and that life was like all other natural challenges. Time would finally get the upper hand. It was a given. Time would also get the better of her. Everything was as it should be. Fanny recognized Alm's words in among her own. It made her feel indebted, in some way obliged.

NOW SHE
UNDERSTOOD
WHAT THE
STAGE WAS
SET FOR

To break up the listlessness of Sunday, Fanny took a bus down to the village, which consisted of a street by the station that was strung with Christmas decorations. There were a few shops, a café, and as many as three hairdressers. The empty postwar industrial buildings by the river recalled a period of optimism, and there were signs of activity in the mechanical workshop, even though it was a Sunday: welding torches flashed and flared inside, producing a bluish luminance.

Before she made her way home again, Fanny decided to see if Alm was in the church. It was late in the evening—the station clock on the yellow brick wall showed half past nine. The fluorescent lights in the bingo hall snapped off and the place emptied with a wave of shouts and laughter, a dog yelped in the distance, freight trains were shunted onto sidings, and a car stopped by a gas pump, but no one got out.

Fanny found Alm in the vestry. He was hanging from a thick, coarse rope. It was tied to the dark-stained beam that ran through the wall and came out by the pulpit. If he had wanted to, he could have swept the floor with his toes, and perhaps in that way stayed on his feet, but now he was hanging in the air, without even swaying. Somehow, the tall, thin man seemed even more ungainly in that exaggerated, vertical position. It looked as though he had grabbed hold of the noose in a desperate attempt to save himself: a firm, useless hold on the rope. Even though it took enormous effort, Fanny had to get him down.

She took the knife that Alm always left on the small desk, the one she had recently used to scrape wax off the candle holder, then she pushed a chair in beside the hanged man, got up on it, and after three resolute cuts with the sharp knife, Alm fell forward, and in falling, head-butted Fanny. The chair was knocked out from under her, and Fanny landed on the stone floor with a thud.

(…)

The light flared and she saw a figure climbing up a transmission tower. It rose up above the three peaks on the far side of the forest where the pine trees squinted at the sun. Who was that fearless person climbing the deadly steel construction? Fanny immediately wanted to be there. She wanted to run, because she had to look this foolhardy person in the eyes.

(…)

And the irregular movements, so formal, so damaged.

(…)

Fanny came to herself, bumped and bruised, and it took all she had to roll over onto her back. Alm lay motionless at her feet. She got up on all fours and tugged at his arm. Her nose was bleeding and there was a cut somewhere above her right eye. Her mouth was full of something viscous that had the sickening taste of metal. For a few minutes she was so groggy and deep in her own pain that it didn't occur to her to phone for help. But she eventually struggled to stand up. Then she staggered out to the vestry, where she fumbled with her phone, and managed in the end to dial the local emergency number. She went back to Alm and lay down beside him. She felt for his pulse. There was no pulse. She put her ear to his chest. No heartbeat. Nothing. Just his twisted face, his pallor that shone faintly in the dim light. There it was, death—it had taken up residency in a body that, more than anything, reminded her of herself. Was this what he had wanted to tell her that evening when he took her for a drive? That ridiculous drive. Was this what he had wanted to warn her about? Fanny imagined that, already then, late that evening, she had become his next of kin, without knowing it. She stroked his head. It was a silly and useless gesture, like refusing to accept a swear word that had already been uttered.

(…)

Thousands upon thousands of sharp tugs.

(…)

Strangely enough, as she fell onto her side, she had the feeling she was rising, not sinking. She thought that whatever it was that might save her would make no demands, but probably would not provide release either. Whatever it was that might save her was whatever it was that had created her. That was her belief. That was what she believed now. But this belief was pure will, will and defiance.

(…)

He no longer resembled a living being.

(…)

It took a minute before Fanny understood that she was in an ambulance. She couldn't face turning to see if Alm was lying beside her. She closed her eyes. Her mother leaned over her. Fanny said she could pick the berries herself, her mother had more than enough to do. Up on the gentle slopes, the bushes blue with berries, you could fill a large pail in under half an hour. Fanny was a hard-working twelve-year-old. She was happy to help, no doubt because she looked forward to the meal; there were always sweet things and all kinds of tempting cakes whenever her mother put on a birthday spread, and, in secret, her father let his daughter try the rhubarb wine, which burned so deliciously in her stomach.

(…)

A mare and foal after a lightning strike.

(…)

The reflection in a glass bottle.

(…)

Sympathy for a small, ill-tempered animal.

(…)

And a soul almost beside itself with love.

(…)

Fanny was rolled down a corridor. The light ran like water from the ceiling. Where was Alm? Where was the minister? To lie like this was a form of reluctant yet absolute abandonment. She hated it. She wanted to look for Alm. She knew where he was. He was in the forest. In the woods by the railway line. The woods she had discovered on her way home from school. That's where Alm was. He had got lost. She wanted to look for him. He was a child. Alm was a child. And if you were a child with a fever, you had to stay away from the forest, if you had a fever, you had to leave the birds and creepie-crawlies and bears in peace, and even if there were no bears among the trees, only moths and little mice and the odd badger, you should still stay away. Because no one there in the dark, inhospitable forest wished you well, not even the ants in their heap or the bats asleep under the thin branches in the depths of a dying spruce.

FORTUNATE CIRCUMSTANCES WITH DEATH AS A CONSEQUENCE

Fanny walked along the main road. She wasn't wearing much, and she had some way to go. The more sensible her thoughts, the greater the urge to do something rash and frivolous. On she walked, she had a goal. Her intention was to find Alm. He was somewhere in the forest. She was certain of it. The woods had appeared that evening when Fanny was on her way home from school. She had only discovered it then. And now that Alm had disappeared, now that he had found a way to leave the ranks of the living, for Fanny it was logical that the two things were connected. She could see him. He was sitting, leaning his back against a small linden tree. His heart was beating as though wrapped in fur and his brain was working to keep his connection with the world open. Fanny was determined to find him. The forest couldn't cover much more than a couple hundred acres. Did you use acres when talking about the size of a forest? Or some other measure? Fanny wasn't sure. She realized that indefatigability was one of her most striking characteristics. She was sure of her case. No explanation was needed. The movement there in the winter dark made everything clear.

She felt a sudden sting in her nose. An insect now, in winter? She wanted to wave it off, but something or someone was holding her arm. And everything was light. A thin shadow flitted in front of her, someone said something, something incomprehensible. She pulled herself loose and hurried to the roadside. In front of her was a stretch of tall grasses, straw and reeds, a small wetland. She had to push her way through to get to the clearing in the forest where Alm was waiting. Something stung her nose again, a needle this time, and the light was all around her, blinding her. She stepped into the frozen grass. The needle was there again: one stitch, then another. Who was it bothering her? Who thought she was mad? Fanny couldn't quite understand the tension between what was driving her forward and what was holding her back. The plants around her were curled up with frost. They crackled. The dark heads of grass reached her face and leaned in to stroke her with their stiff whiskers. She crossed a stream. There was a slow trickle of water on the surface, but under this floating skin lay a body of dark ice, a slain knight in shining armour. A voice said that the cut above the eye needed stitches. And a hand stroked her forehead. Fanny felt the needle pushing in along the edge of her eyebrow, but no pain followed. She was beyond all longitude and latitude. She crawled up the small slope that led to the first trees. The branches snapped. Thick, spiky undergrowth guarded a row of birch trunks. She kicked her way through and immediately entered a colourless twilight. A strange sense of well-being filled her, a warm wave washed through her body. It had been a time of decision, and now that decision had been made, now she was there among the tree trunks, defiant and determined, on her way into or down to the kingdom of death, destined, as it were, as though she were fulfilling a prophesy. And she was fine with that. She was surrounded by a rough landscape. She pulled herself free from the branches that snagged her, pulled herself free from the plastic tubes, making the stand sway, and the clear fluid that was dripping into her sloshed around in its bag.

And later, when all was quiet around her again, she went out into the corridor. The hospital looked abandoned. She saw a clearing between the trees. It was like moving toward something that could be called "once upon a time, a long time ago," something pastoral even though no shepherd had ever set foot there. It was sleeting and the cold downpour reminded Fanny of a kind of happiness she had forgotten or no longer believed. It struck her that the fall, this defeat, was her greatness, now she would do something useful for society, now she would leave everything and everyone to defy the guardians of the kingdom of death, whoever they were, if they even existed.

She found her way to a patch of uneven bog. Waterlogged clusters of grass stood side by side, as if they had bubbled up from the ground. The soil steamed and the silence was like a mystery. It was as though the guards or gods were playing a form of daring intrigue.

Fanny pushed her way through yet another door and came out into another long corridor. The doors to an elevator opened and two nurses rushed out. Fanny walked calmly in and pressed a random button. It turned green. The elevator went down. One of the fluorescent lights on the ceiling flickered. She came down to the basement. A row of enormous washing machines stood there whining, the drums shaking against the concrete floor. Fanny crossed the open floor, walked toward the thickening trees on the other side. A godforsaken province, a forbidden zone. A place where lost souls wander in madness. That is what Fanny thought.

Was she caught in nothingness? Was she now living the life of the dead? No, she could hear what the living said. Whatever it was that held her to the earth was so fragile. And the imagined sleep of the dead was alluring, like the play of light in a trap. And the cold—was that not just a reason to wake up, try to twist away, be released?

But Fanny could not be freed. Fanny had a mission. She had to collect someone from the dead, a departed soul to take home. She thought: the dead also die. They become so incredibly tired. The dead speak to the living without being heard and say things like "Save me from this joy that you find so insufferable" and then they say "Tomorrow is also today."

The forest seemed to swell from within, it expanded. No matter how far she walked, there were still trees, undergrowth, and slopes; the trees got denser again, more knolls, overgrown bushes, a forest that went on and on as far she could see. There were trees that had fallen down. They resembled knights levelled with the ground in past battles. Was that an unexplored sorrow that Fanny glimpsed between the swaying trunks? She stumbled on through the dense tangle of trees and scrambled over thickets and roots. Soon a river appeared in front of her, and without hesitating she waded in. The water gurgled and meandered, its flow was anything but rapid. The cold stung inside her pant legs, but as soon as she came to a deep gorge, she kicked her feet off the ground and started to swim. The water was sticky and shiny and metallic, her strokes regular and strong. She floated in sudden stops and starts under branches that had grown out low and crooked from the bank. The knotty crowns hung over the surface of the water, creating a vault of interwoven branches and leafless vines. Her coat weighed her down. She struggled to take it off and let it float away. For a long time, she drifted drowsily under the hanging trees. The night sky dropped snow on her, flakes that flared in momentary flashes. She thought of Karen, remembered Karen, stumbled across her, like a shameful reminder that she actually existed. Karen. Karen. It was like dreaming that true love was waiting, only to wake up suddenly and see a noble beech tree being felled at the root by a digger. A tree felled at the root.

A stag was grazing in a clearing by the bank. Fanny, shivering, pulled herself up onto dry land and crouched down behind a cluster of reeds. She imagined for a moment that she had the capacity to be happy. It was as though she felt a hunter's sense of duty, and yet forgot to fire the shot.

The stag lifted its head. It stared in Fanny's direction but it didn't pay her any heed, or perhaps it was just a fearless creature. Perhaps it was toying with the idea of attacking her, pursuing her, goring her to death with its splendid antlers. No, it had no idea that she was there. It was a good hiding place, and the wind was not blowing in that direction.

Fanny watched the stag through a gap in the trees. It stood there, majestic, like some royal creature of the tundra flood plains. Then there was a boom in the forest, and the boom was followed by a prolonged rumbling. It sounded like an old generator had been turned on inside a corrugated iron shack. The woodwork creaked, and the forest stiffened, shrunk. The stag ran off, and Fanny ran after it. It bounded over the mires, jumped over the wire fence, and trotted onto the railway track. Fanny fell behind. She was about to give up. But then the stag stopped and stood at the top of a steep slope. It sniffed the air. It looked as though it wanted to turn, as if it intuited a threat, but too late. With straight legs, it careened down the slope and, dazed, ended up on the main road. A grotesque scene unfolded: a car approached. A station wagon. It was bronze-coloured in the golden half-light. It was travelling quickly. Loud music playing inside. A strong bass. The stag was suddenly exposed in the beam of the headlights. Red eyes, tongue out. The driver tried to steer clear, but the car smashed into the guardrail, flipped over, and was thrown back in the same direction. The vehicle skidded on its roof; sparks flew like in a welding shop. It hit the guardrail again and spun round, the headlights frantically sweeping the asphalt. Broken metal trailed behind with a scraping noise until the car stopped spinning. The car tipped forward onto its hood. There was a quiet crunch, after which it ground to a halt on the road. The headlights brightened before burning out. Fanny wanted to run over, but as soon as she had taken a few stumbling steps onto the road, flames burst out of the wheel wells. The driver's door was kicked open and a man crawled out of the car. The flames licked the dark. The man got to his feet and stood watching the hissing, burning car. A couple of cars glided toward the accident. Lumps of dirty snow spat from their back wheels. They stopped. The capsized station wagon soon lay burned out by the guardrail.

The stag was on its way back to the forest. Once again it bounded across the uneven terrain, the unmarked zone. And once again Fanny followed. She came to a place where the trees grew denser. The curtain between the trees was drawn to one side, as though to reveal a sanctuary. There, sitting with his back against one of the tree trunks, was Alm. His head hung down over his chest. Fanny approached the dead man with care. Because even the dead must not be disturbed, disturbed or scared to life.

IN HOSPITAL,
SHE COMPARED
THE TRIALS
SHE HAD BEEN
THROUGH
WITH A DESCENT
INTO THE
UNDERWORLD

Fanny found a couple of armchairs, a table, and sofa at the end of the corridor. Through the window that looked out over the Emergency entrance at the back of the hospital, she saw that the day was dawning. She sat down. The sofa was brown and slippery. A fire extinguisher was mounted on the wall to her left. And to the right, on the floor, was a large glazed pot with a plant in it. One of the nurses appeared with a blanket that she draped over Fanny's shoulders. Gently, she pulled Fanny to her feet and led her back to bed. A few firm words spoken in a level voice, a glass of water that tasted slightly sweet, and the intravenous needle neatly back in place. The nurse checked all the machines by her bed, gave a brief nod, then disappeared.

Fanny squatted down beside Alm. Whispered his name. He lifted his face to her. His eyes were black, impenetrable. He took her hands in his and almost begged for forgiveness. He had always believed that anyone who chose to take their own life should, for the love of God, make it look like an accident. For the love of God. Such annihilation requires meticulous and considerate planning. But someone who takes their own life is the most miserable of souls. A person who takes their own life has no time to waste, no grand plans to ponder, no dreams to realize. Fanny stroked his head. She wanted to know how he, who was dead, could speak, how someone who was dead could be understood by the living, because Fanny was alive, was she not? Fanny was just visiting the realm of the dead. Her mission was clear. She was going to take Alm home. She told him in a clear voice, her mouth to his ear. That was their decision, she explained. He had to get up now and come with her. She knew the way. She knew these parts. He should no longer look back with sorrow.

A nurse wiped the sweat from Fanny's forehead and asked if there was anything she needed. Fanny shook her head. She wanted the nurse to go. To leave the room. Leave the forest. The nurse mustn't disturb her, make the task more difficult than it already was. And as soon as she was alone again, she crept back over to Alm and pulled him to his feet. Together they stumbled across the frozen forest floor, the wintery earth. Fanny first, and Alm a few unsteady steps behind. Alm thought they were dreaming. He said it out loud, almost shouted to her. That he was dreaming about Fanny, dreaming of her, with resignation and regret. He should never have left her, should never have betrayed the trust they had. He had let her down in the most deplorable way. And what if there was no redemption in death? What if he was met on the other side with a smile of derision? Then he was just as powerless.

Fanny stopped and turned toward him. He was supporting himself against the trunk of a thin, upright birch. His body was clearly refusing to obey him now. He collapsed. Imagine if Orpheus had been a girl, he said. Imagine if it was Orphelia or perhaps Orphea. His voice was hoarse, his pitch confused. But he continued, as though there was an obvious connection between his foundering and whatever it was that was troubling him: he had once seen a horse with colic. It was summer. The horse had been frightened by a swarm of bees and run itself into a lather in a paddock, until eventually, terrified and feverish, it had toppled over. A farmhand tried to give it plenty of cold water to drink, to cool it down, but that was just hell for its stomach and intestines. Fortunately the farmer was nearby and came rushing over. The horse has to get up and stand, he shouted, otherwise it'll die. But the way in which the horse was lying, cataleptic and with cramps, made it impossible to move the beast, even for two strong men. The farmer was quick-witted and ran over to the tractor to get his thermos. He pulled a black plastic funnel from his toolbox and pushed the thin end into the horse's ear. Without any hesitation, he poured the warm coffee into the ear canal. The horse rolled over, its hooves scraped the ground, and as if by magic, it jumped up onto all fours.

Fanny heard Karen's voice. Instinctively she opened her eyes, confused. Karen was standing by the bed. Her breathing was calm and steady. No accusations, no demands. Fanny didn't know what to say, how she could express or hold back the joy she felt on seeing her friend. She whispered: "A piece of cloth found in the cupboard in the kitchen." It was like dropping a valuable object onto the floor to get attention. Karen leaned forward and kissed her gently on the mouth, on her dry lips. Fanny asked Karen to wait. Promise that you'll wait for me, she said. Because now she had to go back to the forest, now she had to go back to the other reality one last time, the one that tightened its grip around her wrists, the one that was unsecured and careless. She was now finally going to find out what death was. Her dealings with the truth were going to be carefree from now on. She grabbed Karen's hand, held it briefly, then let go and made her way over to Alm. She saw that it was pointless, his downturned face, as though he was staring down a shaft, and his voice that broke up as he spoke. He managed to stammer that in all his life, he had only ever been ill for two days. As a boy he was often caught off guard by nausea and headaches, but he had only been bedridden because of illness for two days. But now, the most wretched illness of all: this departure with closed eyes. You should know, he said, you should know, dear

Fanny, that when I die (…) the fact that I am now going my own way (…) I find it liberating (…) liberating and unusually captivating.

And in the moment of death: crows rose up from the fields, a spineless insect slipped down into a crack in a cellar floor, and an owl, roosting on a branch, turned its head—the small, fragile skull full of all kinds of finely tuned instincts. The last thing Alm said was that the Madonna of Piedigrotta was the most beautiful of all. She didn't radiate, but she spread light. Fanny carefully laid the dead man on his side, on a bed of rotted moss and leaves. It was so simple. It was like sitting and waiting for the morning sun.

FUTURE
REVELATIONS

Three days later, Fanny and Karen left the hospital and went home to Fanny's. The house was quiet, the rooms were cold. After a light meal, Fanny went to bed. Two days and two nights passed before she left her bed. She dreamed the same dream, the same performance, over and over again: a wet badger had found its way into the kitchen. It padded around, then stopped in the middle of the floor and shook off the snow. Then, frightened by something indeterminable—the dream had no idea what—it ran out with a shrill and angry complaint.

At long last, Fanny awoke. She stretched her arms up in the air, grabbed hold of the headboard, fumbled for nothing, then spotted Karen, who was standing by the window—a delicate silhouette, her arms wrapped around herself. Was she cold or was she protecting herself from some kind of danger? Fanny pushed the duvet to one side, pulled on her pyjama bottoms, found a wool cardigan in the closet, and went to stand beside her friend. Should they go out for a walk? Should they go for a drive up the hill?

They both sat in silence in the car. Fanny settled down and closed her eyes. In her mind's eye, she saw the landscape, knew where they were driving so well: past the woods and the farms, past the sawmill and along the shore. Now they were passing the workshops down by the river, and the bridge that arched over the railway tracks. A bend, and then another, and then they started the long pull up the hill. Fanny opened her eyes. The car sailed through a shady tunnel. Tall spruce trees covered in frost stood at attention, tightly packed, on either side of the gravel track. Only when they came up onto a plateau, with an open view, did Karen stop the car, and they got out.

On the steep slope above them was a huge, snow-covered clearing where all the trees had been felled. The windswept scar was luminous and blinding in the fading light. And below them, the village. Wads of mist hung over the fields and those stretches of road that were lit, cut through the patchwork of fields like yellow lines.

It was soon Christmas. And without showing any dread or joy at the thought of the coming festivities, Fanny pushed back the hood of her coat and turned to Karen. How was it possible? she wondered. This, with Karen. She thought about her all the time.

She wanted to say something about all the expectations in the run-up to Christmas, and then the inevitable disappointment of New Year's Eve. And January and February—they truly were a couple of miserable months. But she said nothing, didn't have time to say anything before a gunshot frightened the birds up from the fields below them. A gun? Or a New Year's firework? The explosion sounded dry in the bitter-cold air. Yes, of course, it was a firework. Fanny pointed to the faint sparks that first went up then showered down in the gloom. No doubt it was some children who just couldn't wait. Another firework went off. Red sparks blossomed and rained down from the heavy sky, slowly, slowly before dying.

The two friends stood there awhile, without saying a word, straight-backed, side by side, shivering in the cold. It started to snow, suddenly the air was thick with snow.

And here, with the white flakes blowing on the wind, the story of Fanny ends. She pushes back her hair. She looks at Karen. And she points to something, but we no longer know what it is. Just snow. There is no blame. There is no innocence. That is how it is for the animals in the forest, and that is how it is for both women and men. To be human means you have no choice. To be human means you must love everything. We are doomed to love everything, so that we don't forget or overlook anything. To overlook even the smallest thing—a handshake, a fond glance between the shelves in a supermarket, the plumage of a nuthatch, or the velvety coat of a shrew—overlooking even the smallest thing can be fatal, it can be the same as losing everything, throwing everything overboard, and losing it forever.

NOTES

The quote "Tobias had dug up a god. A god who had been lying with his scornful smile in the dirt for who knows how long" is taken from Pär Lagerkvist's *Det heliga landet* (1964), translated into English by Naomi Walford (Random House, 1966). The quote "Friendship? Express yourself more clearly. I have never heard that word before" is taken from Jean Giraudoux's play *Amphitryon* 38 (1929), translated into English by S. N. Behrman (1938). The folk tale "The Honest Penny" is from *Asbjørnsen & Moe's Collected Folktales* (1841–1844). "It was a kind of voice that was talking to me…" is an adaptation of a quote from Georges Bernanos's novel *The Diary of a Country Priest* (1936), translated into English by Pamela Morris (Boriswood, 1937). "In hospital she compared the trials she had been through with a descent into the underworld" is a paraphrase of the sentence "And yet I am happy with the certainty I have gained, and I compare the trials I have been through with what in the past was called a descent into the underworld" from Gérard de Nerval's *Aurelie*, translated into English by Geoffrey Wagner (Grove Press, 1959). Reference is also made to Georges Bernanos's *Nouvelle histoire de Mouchette* (1937), translated into English by J. C. Whitehouse (Holt, Rinehart & Winston, 1966); Wolfgang Hildesheimer's *Tynset* (1965), translated into English by Jeffrey Castle (Dalkey Archive Press, 2016); Robert Bresson's film *Mouchette* (1967); and Henry Hobson's film *Maggie* (2015).

© RUNE CHRISTIANSEN

Rune Christiansen is a Norwegian poet and novelist. One of Norway's most important literary writers, he is the author of more than 20 books of fiction, poetry and nonfiction. He has won many prestigious awards, including the 2014 Brage Prize for his bestselling novel, The Loneliness in Lydia Erneman's Life. He is also a professor of creative writing. Rune lives just outside of Oslo, Norway.

KARI DICKSON is a literary translator. She translates from Norwegian, and her work includes crime fiction, literary fiction, children's books, theatre and non-fiction. She is also an occasional tutor in Norwegian language, literature and translation at the University of Edinburgh, and has worked with BCLT and the Writers' Centre Norwich. She lives in Edinburgh.

© ANDY CATLIN

COLOPHON

Manufactured as the first English edition of
Fanny and the Mystery in the Grieving Forest
by Book*hug Press in the fall of 2019

Copy edited by Stuart Ross
Type + design by Tree Abraham

bookhugpress.ca